"It's going to take a lot more than a contract to make me marry you."

Will took a step toward her, his grin widening. "Then tell me what you want, Janie."

This was it. He'd sweep her into his arms and kiss her, ravaging her mouth with his lips. And if he did, Jane might as well start shopping for a white dress. At this rate, there was no way she was going to avoid falling in love with Will McCaffrey again, just as she had all those years ago. But she'd be a fool to put her heart at risk again.

"L-let's suppose for a moment that this contract is legal, which I don't think it is. It was six years ago. You were drunk and I was...under the influence...." She drew a shaky breath. "Why are you doing this, anyway?"

"I just want you to go out to dinner with me tonight. I want to share a bottle of champagne and get to know you all over again."

Jane shook her head, her instinct for self-preservation finally kicking in. "No. I'm not going to date you and I'm not going to marry you!"

Will shrugged and stepped away from her. "Then I guess I'll see you in court."

Dear Reader,

It's Harlequin Temptation's twentieth birthday and we're ready to do some celebrating. After all, we're young, we're legal (well, almost) and we're old enough to get into trouble! Who could resist?

We've been publishing outstanding novels for the past twenty years, and there are many more where those came from. Don't miss upcoming books by your favorite authors: Vicki Lewis Thompson, Kate Hoffmann, Kristine Rolofson, Jill Shalvis and Leslie Kelly. And Harlequin Temptation has always offered talented new authors to add to your collection. In the next few months look for stories from some of these exciting new finds: Emily McKay, Tanya Michaels, Cami Dalton and Mara Fox.

To celebrate our birthday, we're bringing back one of our most popular miniseries, Editor's Choice. Whenever we have a book that's new, innovative, *extraordinary*, look for the Editor's Choice flash. And the first one's out this month! In *Cover Me*, talented Stephanie Bond tells the hilarious tale of a native New Yorker who finds herself out of her element and loving it. Written totally in the first person, *Cover Me* is a real treat. And don't miss the rest of this month's irresistible offerings—a naughty Wrong Bed book by Jill Shalvis, another installment of the True Blue Calhouns by Julie Kistler and a delightful Valentine tale by Kate Hoffmann.

So, come be a part of the next generation of Harlequin Temptation. We might be a little wild, but we're having a whole lot of fun. And who knows—some of the thrill might rub off....

Enjoy,

Brenda Chin
Associate Senior Editor
Harlequin Temptation

KATE HOFFMANN

LEGALLY MINE

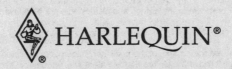

HARLEQUIN®

TORONTO • NEW YORK • LONDON
AMSTERDAM • PARIS • SYDNEY • HAMBURG
STOCKHOLM • ATHENS • TOKYO • MILAN • MADRID
PRAGUE • WARSAW • BUDAPEST • AUCKLAND

ISBN 0-373-69163-7

LEGALLY MINE

Copyright © 2004 by Peggy A. Hoffmann.

This edition published by arrangement with Harlequin Books S.A.

® and TM are trademarks of the publisher. Trademarks indicated with ® are registered in the United States Patent and Trademark Office, the Canadian Trade Marks Office and in other countries.

Visit us at www.eHarlequin.com

Printed in U.S.A.

A NOTE FROM THE AUTHOR...

Sometimes it takes a long time for a story to become a book. And that's certainly been the case with this one! I proposed this idea to my editors about three or four years ago, but the story kept getting pushed aside to make way for other projects, like those Mighty Quinns. But finally the time had come. And during those years, the story that began as a sweet little romance called *The Cupid Contract* evolved into a sinfully sensual tale entitled *Legally Mine*.

What's even more exciting is that I got to write this book for such a special occasion—Harlequin Temptation's twentieth anniversary. It's been wonderful to be a part of Harlequin Temptation's list of authors for ten of those twenty years. From my first book in 1993, *Indecent Exposure,* to this one, I've thoroughly enjoyed being a part of this wonderful series. And I plan to continue writing for it for a long, long time.

So happy birthday, Temptation. And this book is dedicated to all of you readers who've made Harlequin Temptation such a success.

Happy reading!

Kate Hoffmann

Books by Kate Hoffmann

To my readers, who make my stories worth telling.

_____Prologue_____

THE STRAINS OF A CELINE DION ballad echoed through the tiny apartment while the scent of vanilla candles permeated the air. Jane Singleton stepped out of the bubble bath and wrapped herself in her chenille robe, then strolled out to the living room, singing along with the love song.

Everything was perfect. The lights were down low, the champagne was on ice, she'd fluffed up her chintz pillows on the sofa, and the chocolate-covered strawberries were chilling in the refrigerator. It was Valentine's Day and while other girls were fretting over dates and dresses, she was spending the most romantic day of the year pampering herself. After a long, relaxing bath, she was ready to settle in for the evening to enjoy an Audrey Hepburn film festival, starting with her favorite video—_Breakfast at Tiffany's_.

She'd always preferred old-fashioned movie romance to the real thing. In classic movies, love was exciting and overwhelming and...perfect. The meager experience she'd had in her life with the real thing had only proved disappointing. Real romance was uncomfortable and nerve-racking and sometimes downright boring. Her fantasies were so much better. So a solitary

Valentine's Day was far preferable to the other option—paralyzing nerves and unfulfilled expectations.

Besides, what more could a girl known as Plain Jane expect? In high school, she'd been the brainy girl who'd never had a boyfriend, who spent every free minute at her studies. Her social life had revolved around science fairs, academic decathlons and orthodontist appointments. Of course, her hard work had won her a full academic scholarship to Northwestern—where she chose to major in botany. But nothing much had changed since graduation, except for the loss of her braces. Though she'd had a few dates, she still hadn't found the man of her dreams.

Jane picked up her journal and sat down on the sofa, tucking her feet under her. "Another Valentine's Day without a man," she murmured as she wrote. "I'm trying to remain optimistic on this bleak occasion. I just haven't found the right man. The perfect man. My Prince Charming. He's out there somewhere. I just have to be patient and wait for him to find me—like Paul found Holly Golightly."

There *was* one man, a guy who was just about perfect in every way, and even dreamier than George Peppard. When she fantasized about her Prince Charming, it was his face she saw in her dreams. And he lived downstairs, just like Paul had in *Breakfast at Tiffany's*. Actually Paul had lived upstairs, but that was an insignificant point—considering this guy had never looked at her the way Paul looked at Holly. Or the way Prince Charming looked at Cinderella. Or the way a man was supposed to look at a woman he wanted—with lust in his eyes.

Jane shook her head and closed her journal, tossing it onto the coffee table and refusing to surrender to melancholy. Moping around would make this Valentine's Day go from moderately lonely to completely pathetic. Still, it was hard to put him out of her mind. Right now, Will McCaffrey, her Prince Charming, was downstairs getting ready for a romantic night on the town with one of his many girlfriends.

Jane knew he had a big night planned. He'd asked her advice on flowers and she'd sent him to her favorite floral shop with a list of choices for an elegant bouquet. She'd ripped a few restaurant reviews out of the *Chicago Sun Times* and urged him to make a reservation early. And when he'd needed a button sewn on his dress shirt, she'd obliged. She'd even helped him choose the right tie.

"Good old Jane," she muttered. She and Will had been friends since he'd moved in last year, meeting after her bathtub had overflowed and dripped through his apartment ceiling. He'd helped her sop up the mess, she'd offered him freshly baked cookies and a glass of milk in return, and they'd become friends.

It hadn't taken long for her to place him squarely in the middle of her fantasies. And it had taken even less time to realize that he'd never fall for a girl like her. Will preferred tall, willowy blondes with stunning smiles and bodies better suited to wear Victoria's Secret lingerie than comfy chenille robes. His girlfriends were always confident and worldly, and seemed as though they knew exactly how to please a man and weren't afraid to show him. Jane was short and brunette, with a body that looked more boyish than bodacious and a tongue that got tied in knots worthy of any Boy Scout. The only thing about her that had ever pleased a man was her oatmeal-toffee cookies.

With a soft groan, she grabbed the *asplenium nidus* from the coffee table. "What would you do, Lulamae?" she murmured, picking at the foliage of the houseplant. "There has to be a way to make him see that I'm a woman, too. I can be sexy and seductive just like those other girls." But the moment she said it, Jane knew it wasn't true. She'd never be Holly Golightly, she'd always be Jane Goslowly or Jane Goclumsily or Jane Go—

A knock sounded on the door and she frowned as she set down the plant and crawled off the sofa. When she opened the door, her best friend, Lisa Harper, rushed in, a garment bag dangling from her hand.

"You have to help me," she said. "I can't decide on the red dress or the black. I think the red makes my butt look like Montana. And the black one shows entirely too much cleavage. And I wanted to borrow that beaded choker that you bought at Navy Pier last month. Oh, and I need a decent coat to wear. A jacket would look really stupid and make my butt look like Asia." She stopped babbling long enough to look around. "Are you expecting company?"

Jane forced a laugh. "No, just a quiet night alone— me, my plants, Audrey Hepburn and George Peppard."

Lisa groaned. "Oh, not *Breakfast at Tiffany's* again! How many times can you watch that movie?"

"It's timeless," Jane said. "It's the most perfectly romantic movie ever."

"Why don't you come out with me and Roy? You'll eat a fancy meal and drink too much champagne and you'll feel like a new woman."

"This is only your third date. I don't think Roy would appreciate me tagging along." Jane unzipped the garment bag and examined the two dresses. "Wear the red and don't worry about your butt. You can borrow my black cashmere coat. And the necklace is in my jewelry box."

Lisa gave her a quick hug. "You're a peach!" She raced into the bedroom, while Jane settled back on the sofa. Lisa never seemed to be without a date and she'd tried to set Jane up any number of times. But Jane had always felt blind dates were for desperate, love-starved girls who couldn't find a man on their own— and she wasn't about to admit defeat so soon. She still had two and a half years of undergrad left and a whole campus full of possibilities.

"All right," Lisa said as she rushed back through the living room. "Are you sure you won't come? Roy's roommate isn't doing anything tonight. We could make it a double date. He's really cute."

"Maybe another time," Jane said, certain that Roy's roommate—cute or not—would be less than enthusiastic about a last-minute date with her. Besides, Jane's mother had brought her up to believe in the old-fashioned conventions of dating and romance, conventions that required a man to make the first move and a woman to wait patiently until he did.

Lisa shrugged. "All right. But I'll see you tomorrow at the library. We have to study for our cell biology exam."

As Lisa hurried out of the apartment, Jane sighed softly. She'd just have to make a plan to get out and meet more men. She and Lisa could hit one of the many bars near the campus. Or she could get involved in some extracurricular activities, or take a class that didn't include so many science geeks.

"See, things are looking up already," she said as she grabbed the remote. "I've got a plan."

The opening credits had just finished when a sharp rap interrupted her again. Jane rolled her eyes and scrambled off the sofa. "What did you forget?" she asked as she yanked open the door, expecting to find Lisa with another request. Her breath caught in her throat when she looked up into Will McCaffrey's startling blue eyes.

He wore a suit, but his shirt collar was open and his tie askew. His dark hair was mussed, giving him a slightly rumpled look, as if he'd just crawled out of bed. With a gallant gesture, he whipped a huge bouquet of English roses out from behind his back. He frowned as he took in the candlelit room, then shook his head. "I'm sorry. I've interrupted something."

"No, no, it's all right." She took the flowers and stepped aside to let him enter, the distinct scent of whiskey following him inside. When he stumbled slightly, she reached out to grab his arm. "Are—are you all right?"

"No, I'm not all right," he mumbled, throwing himself down on her sofa and covering his eyes with his arm. He held up the nearly empty bottle he carried. "I'm almost out of whiskey and I'm not nearly drunk enough yet." He sat up straight. "Do you have any whiskey?"

"No," Jane said. "I have champagne and some wine coolers. And I think I might have some peppermint schnapps. It—it tastes good in hot chocolate and sometimes, when I can't sleep, I—"

"Bring on the schnapps," he shouted, throwing out his arms. "Let the celebration begin."

"What are we celebrating?"

"My absolute ignorance when it comes to the inner workings of the female mind." He took another swallow of the whiskey. "You're a female, right?"

Jane slowly sat down beside him. "I am." No surprise he had to ask. He'd certainly never noticed. When he looked at her, he saw the shy, unremarkable girl who lived in the apartment above his, the girl with all the houseplants and the sofa full of embroidered pillows and the collection of old movies.

But she'd noticed everything about him—the light in his eyes when he was amused, and the way his hair curled around the collar of his shirt, the tiny dimple in his left cheek when he smiled, and the beauty of his hands. Will McCaffrey had been the subject of countless vivid and detailed romantic dreams, dreams that featured those beautiful hands on her naked body. "What happened? Did you and Amy have a fight?"

"I went to pick her up for dinner and found a note taped to the door. She met someone else, some football player. She was afraid to tell me, afraid to ruin my Valentine's Day. Can you believe that? It's over between us. Yesterday, we were together and now we're... finished."

"I'm sorry," Jane lied.

"Not as sorry as I am." He frowned. "I guess I've been dumped. I've never been dumped before." Will stretched his arms across the back of the sofa, his hand brushing against her nape as he did. "So, this is how it feels."

Jane pressed the roses to her nose, closed her eyes and inhaled, deliberately quelling a satisfied smile. She'd met Amy and found her conceited and self-absorbed and far too obsessed with her figure. "You're probably better off without her."

"Damn straight."

She risked a glance at him, allowing her gaze to take in his profile, the chiseled jaw and the sensuous mouth and the impossibly straight nose. His eyes were closed and for a moment, she thought he might be asleep. But then he shifted slightly. "There's a perfect girl out there for you, Will. You just have to find her. She might be closer than you think."

"Amy was perfect."

"No, she wasn't. Because she didn't love you as much as I—" Jane swallowed hard. "As I think you deserve to be loved."

Will opened his eyes and looked at her. "You're sweet, Janie. You always know what to say to make me feel better."

He said it as if the thought had just occurred to him. A warm flush crept up her cheeks and she dropped her gaze to the flowers.

"You are," Will insisted, curling his arm around her to toy with a strand of hair that brushed her cheek. "You're just about the sweetest girl I've ever known."

In a heartbeat, he'd pulled her into his arms, giving Jane a fierce hug, fueled more by whiskey than passion. Her first impulse was to pull away, but then she realized this might be the opportunity she'd been hoping for. Sure he was drunk, but a girl had to take her breaks where she got them. So she slipped her arms around his waist.

When he drew back, he stared down at her, his gaze skimming her features like a silent caress. Jane held her breath, waiting for him to make the next move, praying that he'd just throw caution to the wind and kiss her. Her heart slammed in her chest and she was certain he could hear it. Every nerve in her body jangled with anticipation—of the warmth of his lips on hers, of the taste of him when his tongue invaded her mouth, of the feel of his hands on her naked skin.

Will smiled and drew his thumb across her lower lip, his eyes fixed on her mouth. But suddenly, his mood shifted. "I'm never going to find anyone," he said, letting his hands fall away. He sank back into the cushions and took another swallow of the whiskey. "I'm twenty-four years old. My father expects certain things from me. He expects me to get my law degree this spring and then he expects me to work for the family business. I've got so many ideas for the company and someday, I'm going to run the whole show, just you watch. McCaffrey Commercial Properties is going to be my company and it's going to be the biggest in Chicago." Will drew a ragged breath. "And he expects me to find a wife and start a family."

"Today?" Jane asked.

"No. But soon," Will said.

"You have plenty of time."

Will shook his head. "I've dated a lot of girls, Jane. And in the beginning, it always seems like I've found the one. But then something happens and I realize she's not exactly what I'm looking for." He drained the bottle of whiskey and leaned forward to set it on the coffee table. "You know, Amy really had ugly feet. And when she laughed, it sounded like she had the hiccups."

"Can I get you something more to drink?"

He turned back to her and sent her a sleepy smile. "You're sweet." Will reached out and cupped her cheek in his palm. "Have I ever told you that?"

"Yes, you have," Jane reminded him, slightly impatient. Not that she didn't like hearing it.

"But you are," he said. "You're always there for me, Janie. You care about me."

"You're my friend," Jane murmured.

He leaned forward and when his lips brushed hers, a startled sigh slipped from her throat. He took the sound as surrender and captured her mouth in a kiss so unexpected, yet so stirring Jane felt her heart swell. His tongue teased hers and she knew she'd never been kissed like this before. There had been boys in her past, clumsy, fumbling boys who couldn't kiss, much less voice a romantic sentiment. But she'd never had a man, a man like Will McCaffrey who could stir this desire she hadn't known she possessed.

As the kiss spun out, her mind whirled with questions. Was this the beginning of something between them? Had he also harbored a secret crush? Or was this just a side effect of all the whiskey he'd drunk? As she wrapped her arms around his neck, Jane realized it didn't make any difference. Will McCaffrey was kissing her! And if she thought too much about it, she might just wake up and find out this was all a dream.

And just as quickly as the kiss began, it ended. Will straightened and stared down at her, an earnest look in his eyes. "I have a really good idea. If I'm not married by the time I'm thirty and you're still single, would you marry me?"

Jane gasped, her heart leaping into her throat. She'd imagined this moment so many times in a wide variety of scenarios, with a wide range of potential fiancés. But she'd never imagined *this* situation—her dressed in an unflattering chenille robe, him drunk and despairing over another woman. "You—you're not serious," she said, her voice cracking. "You're drunk and you're upset with Amy."

"I am serious," Will insisted, his words slurred by the liquor. He shoved up from the sofa and crossed the room to her desk. "I need paper."

"In the top tray," Jane said. "Are you going to write Amy a note?"

When he returned to her side, he had a pen in his hand as well. "Nope. I'm going to write a contract. An agreement between us that if you're free and I'm free, we'll get married."

"What? You're just going to write it down and it will be a contract?"

"Sure. I got an *A* in my contracts course. I can write a basic agreement. It's simple. If we're both free, then we'll get married."

"Don't we need a witness or a notary or something?"

"We'll just have to find a witness," Will murmured. He reached for the whiskey bottle and when he noticed it was empty, he dropped it on the floor.

Jane sat next to him on the sofa, her feet tucked beneath her, as she watched him write out the contract. She tried to read his expression, to figure out where the spontaneous proposal had come from. But the more she thought about it, the more she realized the proposal was all just a silly exercise to soothe his bruised ego.

As he worked, Jane wandered into the kitchen and found the bottle of champagne she'd put in the ice bucket. A marriage contract was probably something worth celebrating, she mused, as she popped the cork. She filled a champagne flute and guzzled the entire glass, hoping that it might give her a bit more courage. There had to be a way to get him to kiss her again.

As she passed the window in the kitchen, Jane caught her reflection and groaned softly. The chenille robe made her look like a sausage, tied in the middle. She might attract a few hungry Germans with an outfit like that, but Will expected more. She took the clip out of her hair and let it tumble down around her face, then pinched her cheeks. Changing wasn't an option, so instead, she loosened the tie of her robe until the neck draped open a bit more.

Drawing a deep breath, Jane grabbed a second champagne flute and walked back to the sofa. "Would you like some champagne? Or I could get you something else."

He glanced up at her and smiled, his gaze dropping to her cleavage. Instinctively Jane followed his gaze and noticed she really didn't have anything to show. Her hand flitted to her robe and she drew it back together again, embarrassed by her feeble attempt at seduction. She went to sit down beside him, but a soft rap at the door stopped her.

Will glanced up. "Are you expecting someone?"

Jane shook her head, frustrated by the interruption. When she opened the door, she found their landlady, Mrs. Doheny, standing in the hall, a paper plate filled with frosted heart-shaped cookies in her hands. "Happy Valentine's Day, Jane," she said with a cheerful smile.

"I—I'm almost done," Will called. "Who's at the door?"

Mrs. Doheny peered over Jane's shoulder. "Is that Will? Will McCaffrey, I just dropped a plate of cookies at your door. I thought you'd be out romancing one of your pretty girlfriends tonight." She gave him a little wave. "Happy Valentine's Day, William!"

"Thanks, sweetie," he said, sending the landlady a wide smile. "I can't let Valentine's Day pass without a kiss from my best girl."

At first, Jane thought Will was talking about her. But then Mrs. Doheny clucked her tongue and bustled inside. When she reached the sofa, Will stood and planted a kiss on the old woman's cheek. A blush stained her pale skin. Even the widow Doheny couldn't resist him, Jane mused. Will could charm the orthopedic stockings off any eighty-year-old.

"Mrs. Doheny, you're just in time," Will said, drawing her down to sit next to him. "You can be our witness."

"Witness? To what?" She set the cookies on the coffee table.

"Just a little agreement between me and Jane," he explained. "You just need to watch us sign and then sign yourself. Jane, you're first." He handed her the pen and then the paper, covered with his lazy scrawl.

What had begun as a silly joke suddenly seemed dead serious. Was this really a contract? Was it legal? She glanced down at the text, but then brushed aside her concerns. This *was* a joke. Besides, even if the contract was real, Will was drunk. Even she knew a person couldn't sign a contract when they were drunk. And there was no way Will McCaffrey was going to show up in six years demanding she marry him. After all, he was...well, he was Will McCaffrey and she was Jane Singleton. Enough said.

"Are you sure you did this right?" she teased, trying to keep her tone light. "Once I tie you up in legalities, I don't want you to get away on a technicality."

"It's all there," he said, watching her put pen to paper. "Aren't you going to read it before you sign?"

"No, I trust you." She scribbled her name on the bottom and handed the contract back to him. "Now you."

Will stared at the contract for a long moment and Jane wondered if he was already reconsidering, thinking about Amy, about how he might get her back and persuade her to marry him. Then he quickly signed it and handed it to Mrs. Doheny. She did the same, with a flourish and a little giggle. "What am I signing?"

Will took the paper and pen from her. "Nothing important. Just a little agreement between me and Jane."

Mrs. Doheny nodded, then stood up and headed for the door. "Well, I have more cookies to deliver. I'll see you two later. Toodles!"

When she'd closed the door behind her, Jane sighed softly, almost afraid to look at Will. She touched her lips, her mind returning to the kiss they'd shared. She could either act like it hadn't happened or she could...she *could.* Jane reached down for the tie to her robe. She could slip out of the unflattering garment and see what happened. Her fingers fumbled at the knot and Jane felt the robe gape open as she turned to face him. Oh, God, her mother would never approve, but if she waited for Will to make another move, she might have to wait forever. And though she'd always considered herself to be a bit old-fashioned, this situation called for a woman who was thoroughly modern, a woman who could make her needs known and get them satisfied at the same time.

Will's gaze skimmed her body as she approached and then he suddenly jumped up from the sofa. "I've got to go, too," he murmured.

Jane froze, her fingers still fumbling with the tie to her robe. "Sure," she said. "Right. It's getting late and I—well, I have—" She swallowed hard. "Plans." Jane quickly hurried to the door and yanked it open.

He smiled, carefully folding the contract and slipping it into the breast pocket of his jacket. Then he pulled out his wallet and handed her a five-dollar bill. "This is consideration," he said.

Confused, Jane took the money. "That is considerate of you," she said. "I can always use laundry money."

"No, it makes the contract binding." His gaze caught hers and for a long moment, it held. Jane wondered what was going through his mind, if he was remembering how it felt to kiss her—or how it might feel to do more. "I guess I'll see you later, Janie."

"Later," she repeated.

When she closed the door behind him, Jane leaned back against it, biting her bottom lip to keep it from trembling. If she'd only been smarter, or prettier, or sexier, she could have convinced him to stay. She could have lured him into her bed and they could have made love all night long. Then, for the first time in her life, she could have had a Valentine's Day worth remembering.

She drew a ragged breath and wandered back to the sofa. Picking up the remote, she settled back onto the sofa. Suddenly her evening seemed empty and pathetic compared to the memory of the kiss they'd shared.

A tear slipped from the corner of her eye and she brushed it away, forcing her lips into a smile. "Well, at least I can say I was kissed on Valentine's Day," she murmured. "Even if he doesn't remember it in the morning."

1

"WHY CAN'T YOU BE MORE LIKE Ronald? He's the son I never had."

Will McCaffrey stifled a groan and clutched the back of one of the guest chairs in his father's office. "You had a son, Dad. You still do. Me."

"Lately, Ronald's more like a son than you are."

Hell, he hated this conversation. He'd been through this with his father at least once a month for the past two years, ever since Jim McCaffrey had decided to retire. Choosing a successor had come down to two choices—Jim's dull but dependable son-in-law, Ronald. Or Will, who hadn't quite lived up to paternal expectations.

"Tell me," Will countered, "was Ronald the son who doubled this company's net worth in just four years? Did Ronald go out and get us the Winterbrook project or the West Washington development deal?" He paused for effect. "No, wait. That was your other son. The son who has worked his ass off for this company. Now what was his name?"

Will served as corporate counsel and executive vice president for McCaffrey Commercial Properties, but he'd worked his way up from the bottom, starting when he was just a junior in high school and ending in a permanent position when he graduated from law school. He had the brains and the drive to continue what his father had begun thirty years ago, to make it even better. What he didn't have was a wife—which for some bizarre reason, known only to his father, would instantly turn him into CEO material.

Just the thought of marriage made him nervous. He understood the concept and its allure, and he even believed in happily-ever-afters. He'd seen his parents' marriage and knew it was possible. But he also knew that happiness could be snatched away in just a blink of an eye.

"Ronald is not prepared to run this company," Will said in an even tone, picking up an old copy of *Business Week* and flipping through it casually. "He's too conservative, he has to triple-think every decision and then half the time he makes the wrong choice. Have you ever watched him order lunch? 'I'll have the salmon—no wait, how is the strip steak? Well, maybe I should have a salad. Has anyone tried the veal chop?' It's a wonder the guy hasn't starved by now."

"No wonder at all," his father countered. "He has a wife at home who makes him dinner every night."

"Why does a wife, three children and a house in the suburbs qualify him to run this company?"

"He's settled. He's made choices in his life and he has responsibilities to look out for, namely your sister and my grandchildren. I don't have to worry that he'll run off to Fiji with the next stewardess he meets."

"They're called flight attendants. And who says I can't take a vacation every now and then?"

His father scowled. "You called on Tuesday afternoon to say you wouldn't be in to work on Monday morning."

"I got confused with time change. That whole thing with the International Date Line is very complicated."

His father sighed. "I know you have your wild oats to sow, Will. But life comes down to choices. You can't stay a bachelor the rest of your life."

Will felt his frustration grow. Why did it always have to come down to this same old argument? It wasn't as if he was avoiding marriage, he just hadn't found the right woman—the perfect woman. Hell, he'd never driven the same car for more than a year. How was he supposed to choose a mate for the next fifty years? "Not everyone is going to have what you and Mom had," he muttered.

Just the thought of his mother brought a twinge of grief, even after all these years. Laura Sellars Mc-Caffrey had died when Will was just twelve and his sister ten, and since then it had been just the three of them. After her death, Jim McCaffrey had thrown himself into work, turning his small real-estate brokerage into one of Chicago's most successful commercial developers. In the process, he'd left his two children to grieve on their own, and to raise themselves.

Melanie had retreated behind the responsibilities of running the household, learning to be the perfect substitute for her mother. When she was barely twenty, she'd married her high-school sweetheart, Ronald Williams. He'd come to work for the family business, she'd joined the garden club and, together, they'd produced three perfect children.

Will had had the opposite reaction to his mother's

death. He could barely stand to stay in the house, memories of her infused every room. He'd found comfort in friends, first his buddies from school and then, as he'd grown older, pretty girls. Somewhere along the line, the girls had become women, always bright and very beautiful. And though he'd always assumed he'd find a wife someday, the women he dated always seemed to fall short.

"What do you want me to do?" he asked. "Marry someone I don't love just so I can say I'm married?"

"You've introduced me to six or seven of your girlfriends, any one of whom would have made you a decent wife. You need to grow up and decide what's important to you—your future or the next beautiful woman to cross your path." Jim McCaffrey crossed his arms over his chest. "I'm going to retire in April. Either you get your personal life in order or you'll be taking orders from Ronald."

Will's jaw clenched and he decided to make his escape while he could, before his father brought up more reasons why Will would never occupy the corner office and he was goaded into a knock-down-drag-out fight. Maybe he ought to just forget about a future with the family business. He was a good lawyer. Hell, he'd even taught a few seminars at his alma mater. And he couldn't count the number of law school buddies who called each week asking his opinion on some matter of real-estate law. He'd had job offers from most of the major firms in the city over the past few years, why not just start fresh?

He retreated to his office, closing the door behind him. When he'd settled into his well-worn chair, Will groaned softly. How could he consider leaving? This business was in his blood—the excitement of putting a deal together, of anticipating the problems and smoothing them over, of watching an empty piece of land become a vital part of the city. He'd helped build the business. By rights, it should be his someday.

Will snatched up the messages his secretary had placed on his desk, but his mind was still occupied with his father's demands. Love and marriage had been so easy for his sister. She'd known exactly who she wanted to spend the rest of her life with by the time she was twenty. He was thirty years old and he wasn't any closer to finding Miss Right.

The way his father talked, it all sounded so simple. Find a woman, fall in love, get married and live happily-ever-after. But love had never come easily to Will. Even after all these years, he could still remember the way his mother had looked at his father, as if he could do no wrong. The gentle teasing way his father had made his mother laugh. The secret whispers and stolen kisses when they'd both thought the children weren't looking. That was love—and Will had never once experienced even a small measure of that kind of devotion.

A knock sounded on the office door and Will glanced up to see his secretary, Mrs. Arnstein, walk inside. After he had dated and broken up with three separate secretaries, his father had decided to choose a secretary for him, a woman who would defy temptation. And Mrs. Arnstein was just that. A former Army drill sergeant, the woman was coldly efficient and painstakingly proper. She also outweighed Will by a good twenty or thirty pounds.

"I have your mail," she said. "The contracts came for the Bucktown condo project. And the estimates came in for the DePaul renovation." She held up a glossy magazine. "And your Northwestern alumni magazine came. You're listed in the class notes this month."

Will took the offered magazine. "How did they find out about me?"

"They sent a questionnaire a few months ago. You told me to fill it out for you. You didn't have time."

The alumni notes took up the last six or seven pages of the magazine. Will scanned the columns for his name, then realized they were listed by year of graduation. But as he flipped back to the previous page, a familiar name caught his eye.

"Did you find it?" Mrs. Arnstein asked.

"No." He quickly closed the magazine. "I'll look for it later. I have work to do."

The moment his secretary closed the door behind her, he snatched the magazine up and returned to the page. "Jane Singleton, B.S. Botany, 2000," he read out loud. "Jane runs her own landscape business, Windy City Gardens, and has designed and installed a wide variety of residential and commercial gardens in the Chicago area."

He hadn't thought about Janie Singleton for—God, how long had it been? Five, maybe six years? "Now *she* would have made a perfect wife," he murmured. "She was sweet and attentive and—" He paused, memories flooding his brain. Will slowly pushed out of his chair and crossed his office to the bookshelves that lined one wall, scanning the volumes until his found his contracts text from law school. Holding his breath, he opened the front cover.

It was right where he'd put it years ago. He'd come across it when he'd unpacked his books after law school and had almost tossed it out. But then he'd tucked it inside the cover where it had stayed until this moment, just a silly memory of a night long ago.

Will unfolded the paper and slowly read it, surprised that he'd managed to write a pretty decent contract with such limited practical experience. The terms were clear and he'd covered all contingencies. Hell, if the contract was challenged in court, it might just hold up. An idea flashed in his brain and he pushed it aside. "No, I can't."

He dropped the contract onto his desk and turned to his computer to get back to work. But the more he thought about it, the more he realized that he might have an easy solution to all his problems. Janie Singleton. She was exactly the kind of woman his father would love. And if his father saw that Will was dating an "appropriate" woman, then perhaps he'd soften his stance, maybe delay his decision until Will did find a wife.

He picked up the phone and dialed his secretary's extension. "Mrs. Arnstein, I need a phone number and address for Windy City Gardens. It's a landscape contractor here in Chicago. And could you see if you can find a home phone number for a Jane Singleton? She probably lives in the city."

He sat on the edge of his desk, rereading the blurb in the magazine. A landscape contractor, that's what she'd become. She'd always loved plants, so it seemed like a natural fit. And knowing her drive and determination, no doubt the business was a success.

He could only speculate on her personal life. The newsletter listed her maiden name, but that didn't mean she hadn't stumbled across the man of her dreams in the past six years. After all, Jane was smart and pretty and she'd make any man a great wife.

He picked up the paper and let his gaze skim over the words of the contract. Though it was written well, any judge with half a brain would toss it out in court. Still, it was a place to start, an excuse to call Jane and catch up on old times. If he was lucky, he could rekindle his relationship with her and just see where it went.

The soft ring of his phone interrupted his thoughts. "Mr. McCaffrey, I have an address for Windy City Gardens. It's 1489 North Damen in Wicker Park." Will scribbled down the address and the phone number as his secretary read them. "I couldn't find a home phone. There were seven J. Singletons but no Janes."

"Fine."

Will ripped the address from the legal pad, stuffed it into his pocket and grabbed his keys. As he walked out, he stopped at Mrs. Arnstein's desk. "Cancel my appointments for this afternoon."

"You're not going to Fiji again, are you?" she asked, arching her eyebrow.

He smirked. "No. Just over to Wicker Park. If there's an emergency, you can get me on my cell phone."

The midday traffic was light on the drive to the Wicker Park neighborhood, and fifteen minutes later, Will pulled up across the street from a small office building. A sign in a street-level window indicated he was at the right place. Even so, he couldn't seem to get out of the car.

"This is crazy," he murmured. "She could be married or involved. I can't just show up and expect her to be thrilled to see me." He reached down to put the car into gear, then froze as he saw a figure step out the front door of the building. Will recognized her immediately, her dark hair and delicate frame, the profile that defined the word "cute." She stood on the sidewalk and talked with a slender blonde who seemed vaguely familiar. A few moments later, they walked in different directions, Jane crossing the street and heading toward his car.

Without thinking, he pushed the door open and stepped out. "Jane?" She stopped and glanced around, her gaze finally coming to rest on him. Will leaned over the top of the car door. "Jane Singleton?"

"Will?" A smile broke across her face and he felt his heart warm. She was happy to see him. "My gosh, Will McCaffrey, you're the last person I expected to run into today."

"I thought it was you," he said, trying to feign total surprise. Will stared at her. It was the same Jane, but she was different. Features that had once been a bit plain had changed into something quite striking, not cute at all, but beautiful. She'd been a nineteen-year-old girl when he'd last seen her. Now, she was definitely a woman.

"What are you doing here?" Jane asked.

He slammed the car door and circled the hood to stand in front of her. "I...I was just heading...up the street, to a restaurant." Will reached out and before he realized what he was doing, he'd grabbed her hand. He hadn't meant to touch her, but now that he had, he realized how much he'd missed her.

For two years, Janie had been a constant in his life, a friend who'd been there whenever he'd needed her. A sliver of guilt shot through him. And he'd never taken the time to thank her, or even to return the favors she'd so eagerly done for him. He stared down at her hand and slowly rubbed his thumb along her wrist. "It's really good to see you, Janie."

She shifted nervously and tugged her hand away. "What restaurant?"

"What? Oh, I don't know the name," he said. "I just know it's on this block." He smiled. "You look great. It's been a long time. What have you been up to?"

"A long time," she repeated. "Yes, it has. Six years almost. I think the last time I saw you was the day you graduated from law school. We were going to keep in touch but then...well, you know how it goes. I got so busy and..."

"I'm sorry we didn't," Will said, the sentiment sincere.

"Me, too."

As he stood in front of her, he fought the urge to touch her again, to drag her into his arms and reassure himself that it was really Jane. Memories of her flooded his mind, memories that he hadn't even recalled storing away. The long, thick lashes that ringed her dark eyes. The perfect shape of her mouth, like a tiny Cupid's bow. And the scent of her, like fresh air and spring flowers. "You know, I don't have to be at the restaurant for a half hour. Maybe you and I could have a cup of coffee?"

She stepped back, as if the invitation caught her by surprise. "I—I can't," Jane said. "I—I'm late for an appointment. But it was really nice seeing you, Will."

"Well, then dinner," Will insisted. "Whenever you like. How about this weekend? There's this terrific new Asian restaurant downtown. You like Asian food, don't you?"

"This weekend won't work," Jane said. "Listen, it was great seeing you again."

"Lunch?" Will asked. "You must eat lunch."

"I never have time." She gave him a little wave and rushed off down the sidewalk, looking back just once.

Will stood at the car, stunned at how quickly it was over. He watched until she turned a corner. "Well, that was just great," he muttered. "If I can't talk her into a cup of coffee, how am I going to convince her to date me?" A soft curse slipped from his lips, but then he remembered the contract. He'd just try again—and again, if he had to. And if Jane Singleton continued to resist his charms and refuse his invitations, he'd just have to use the only weapon he had—the law.

"MAYBE WE COULD ASK FOR an extension on the rent."

Jane Singleton pressed her fingers to her temples and stared at the spreadsheet program on her computer, knowing that the suggestion wouldn't make any difference. The columns of numbers blurred in front of her eyes and she caught herself daydreaming again, her mind wandering back to her encounter with Will McCaffrey last week.

He'd looked so good, the same, but different, more polished and sophisticated. When she'd first seen him standing next to his car, Jane had been certain he was a figment of her imagination. But he had been real, and after all these years, he still had the capacity to send her pulse into overdrive and turn her brain into mush.

Overwhelmed and exasperated by her reaction, she'd made a quick escape. Though she'd once harbored a secret crush on Will McCaffrey, she'd finally managed to put her fantasies aside. She was a grown woman now, not some silly schoolgirl.

Still, Will wasn't making it easy. He'd called three times since their chance meeting to ask her out and over and over again, she'd come up with a litany of feeble excuses. She'd been tempted, but Jane knew she could never trust herself around him—he could make her fall in love all over again with just a simple smile.

"Jane!"

She jerked up and placed her palms on her desk. "What? I was listening. The numbers just don't add up. Right. I can see that. We're not going to have enough to keep the office."

Lisa Harper shook her head. "All right. What's wrong? You've been distracted all morning. I know we're under a lot of pressure here, but you're always so focused at times like these. Tell me what's wrong."

Lisa had been her friend since freshman year in college and her business partner since they'd founded Windy City Gardens after they'd graduated. But Lisa had spent too many evenings listening to Jane babble about Will McCaffrey to have him reappear in their conversations again. "It's nothing," Jane murmured.

"Tell me."

"You won't like it," Jane warned her.

"You're my best friend. You're supposed to tell me every little detail about your life. It's part of the deal. We talk about highly personal matters, you insist that I look skinny in everything I wear, you encourage me to eat more chocolate because it's good for my skin, and you—"

"If I tell you, you have to promise this isn't going to become a thing."

"A thing?"

"Yeah. Whenever we discuss my personal life and you have an opinion, you want to talk about it over and over and analyze it. And then, once *you've* decided what *I* should do, you won't let up until I do it. If I tell you this, you have to promise to just drop it, all right?"

"Promise," Lisa said, drawing a cross over her heart.

"I saw Will McCaffrey last week."

Lisa's expression turned from genuine interest to outright disbelief. "Oh, no. Not again. You haven't mentioned his name for nearly two years. We are not bringing him back into conversation. The man has ruined you for all men."

"How is that?"

"Because you haven't met one man in the past six years that you haven't compared to Will McCaffrey. You'd think the guy was some kind of god. He's just a jerk who never appreciated you while he was around."

"He was right across the street. He was getting out of his car and I was on my way to the Armstrong appointment and there he was, just standing there."

Lisa covered her ears. "La, la, la, la, la. I'm not listening. I can't hear you."

Jane reached out and pulled Lisa's hands from her ears. "All right. I won't talk about him. Let's get back to business." She drew a deep breath. "It's November. Even if we bring in ten new contracts for the spring, we're not going to get paid until at least April. We knew the risks when we decided to go into the landscaping business in Chicago. Gardens don't grow in the winter."

"So what did he say?" Lisa asked.

"I think our only option is to diversify. We'll do Christmas decorations. Put up outdoor lights, decorate trees. We can call some of our competitors, see if they're too busy. They could subcontract some of their jobs to us."

"Is he still as handsome as he always was?" Lisa wriggled in her chair. "He always was a hottie. And he knew it, too. I guess it's too much to hope that he's gained fifty pounds and has developed a bad case of acne."

"We cut costs as much as we can," Jane continued, sending Lisa a quelling glare. "We get rid of the office and transfer the phone. We'll have to keep the garage for equipment storage. And we call all our past and present clients and offer up our services as Christmas decorators. And then we find a place that will give us a cut rate on twinkle lights." A tiny smile was all that Jane could muster. There was one good thing about being an eternal optimist. Even in the face of impending disaster, she could keep her wits about her. But it wasn't easy when things looked this bad. "Even with the Christmas jobs, I'm still not going to be able to make my rent. I'm two months behind and I have less than one hundred dollars in my checking account."

"Can we please talk about Will?" Lisa pleaded.

Jane eyed her business partner. "I thought you didn't want to hear about him."

"All right. I admit. I'm curious and we might as well get it out of the way so we can get down to business."

It didn't take much encouragement for Jane to spill the beans. She'd been thinking about him nonstop for nearly six days and she felt as if she were about to burst into flames unless she put her thoughts into words. "He looked different. Handsome and sexy. And respectable. He was wearing a suit that made his shoulders look so broad, and his hair was shorter. But he's still just as confident and charming as ever."

"What did he say?"

"I really can't remember. The moment he touched me I just—" Jane fluttered her fingers around her face. "I got all flustered. He asked me out, first to coffee, then to dinner and then to lunch. You would have been proud of me. I said no and then I got out of there before I starting drooling all over him."

"You turned him down."

"Yes. And not just then. He's called me three times this past week to ask me out again. But I'm strong. I've decided going out with him would be a big mistake and I'm determined never to see him again. It was just a chance meeting and it's over."

"So he still did it to you," Lisa muttered. "He still made your heart race and your palms sweat?"

"No," Jane cried. "Well, maybe, a little. But I'm a different person now. I'm not that silly girl who filled up journal after journal with her fantasies about him. I'm not that girl who wasted sleep dreaming about him. Not anymore," she lied. Although there had been more than a few very vivid dreams over the past nights, dreams that had featured a tall, dark man who looked a lot like Will. "Besides, I have a boyfriend."

"You mean David?"

"Yes. Last month we had two dates. He took me to that play and we went to see a movie together. And we had dinner afterward. He's sweet and polite and handsome. The kind of man I can trust. The kind of man who won't break my heart."

David Martin was an architect who had first contacted Windy City Gardens to do the landscaping for a home he'd designed. They'd worked with him on six other projects and he and Jane had formed a friendship. Though David seemed happy with the occasional date, Jane had always hoped that their relationship would progress to something a bit more intimate than a chaste peck on the cheek at the end of the evening.

"I still think he's gay," Lisa said, her voice tinged with suspicion.

"He is not! He's just well-dressed and well-groomed. Just because he pays particular attention to his appearance doesn't make him gay."

"Don't you remember what brought you together? Your mutual love of Celine Dion and Audrey Hepburn."

"We share common interests. He's a sweet, sensitive, understanding man—unlike Will McCaffrey who wouldn't think of sitting through an Audrey Hepburn double feature."

"Back to Will McCaffrey again," Lisa murmured.

"If I had a choice between David Martin and Will McCaffrey, I'd choose David every day of the week and twice on Sundays."

The bell on the front door rang and they both turned to watch a messenger walk inside. "Here we go," Lisa said, deftly changing the subject. "This nice man is bringing us new business, I can feel it. Or maybe he has an envelope filled with cash."

"Are you Jane Singleton?" the messenger asked.

Lisa pointed to Jane. "That's her."

"I'm supposed to deliver this to you personally and then make sure you read it."

Jane took the envelope, noting the stamp on the front. "Personal and Confidential," she read.

"Who's it from?"

"There's no return address." She tore into the envelope and pulled out a photocopy of a handwritten document. As she began to read, she slowly recognized the handwriting. And when her gaze dropped to the bottom of the page and found her own signature, Jane gasped. "Oh, my God."

"What is it?"

Jane handed Lisa the contract and read the cover letter. "In the matter of the contract between William A. McCaffrey and Jane Singleton, we must discuss the satisfaction of terms as soon as possible. I've scheduled a meeting at my office for tomorrow at 10:00 a.m. Sincerely, William McCaffrey, Attorney at Law."

"We're doing Will McCaffrey's garden? Gee, Jane,

I'm impressed. You managed to pitch him a project while avoiding him at the same time?"

"Read the contract. This doesn't have anything to do with a garden. This is about...marriage."

Lisa's eyes went wide. "Marriage? Like in 'husband and wife, till death do us part'?" She quickly scanned the contract, then glanced up at Jane, a stunned expression on her face.

"It was a joke," Jane said. "He was depressed and I was...vulnerable and he suggested if neither of us was married by the time he was thirty, then we'd...oh, God. I'd forgotten all about this. How could I forget about this?"

"Do you have any return message?" the messenger asked impatiently.

"No," Jane said, forgetting he was still standing there. "Wait, yes." She stepped up to the young man and poked a finger into his chest. "You can tell Will McCaffrey that he has a lot of nerve digging up this silly contract. I'm not going to marry him. I'm not going to date him." She gave the guy another poke. "And you can tell him if he thinks I'm still the same love-starved, weak-willed, stupid little girl who kissed him that—" Jane bit her bottom lip. "Never mind. I'll tell him myself."

The messenger nodded, then hurried out of the office, clearly unnerved by her outburst.

"When did you kiss Will McCaffrey?"

"Valentine's Day, February 14, 1998. Six years ago. He was drunk. And I was completely out of my mind." She grabbed the contract from Lisa. "This can't be legal. Look at it. It's handwritten. And this doesn't even look like my signature."

"*Is* that your signature?" Lisa asked.

"Yes."

"Then I think it might be legal."

Jane felt a warm flush creep up her cheeks and her stomach churned with nerves. "I guess I'm going to have to get a lawyer."

"Either that or marry Will McCaffrey," Lisa chirped.

JANE SMOOTHED HER HANDS over the front of her skirt, working out a wrinkle that had developed on the ride downtown. She'd spent most of the morning trying to decide what to wear to her meeting with Will. She'd begun with the sexy choices, anxious to prove that she wasn't the same clumsy girl that he'd once known, that she'd grown into a confident, attractive woman who didn't need a contract to find a husband.

But she'd discarded those outfits for more conservative choices, a tailored blazer and pants with a silk blouse and elegant jewelry, something to counter his power suit. But that choice hid every trace of femininity, so she traded the pants for a pencil-slim skirt and heels, a wardrobe choice that she rarely employed.

After dressing, she'd fussed with her hair, trying to train the waves into something more subdued. She'd finally given up on the tousled curls and carefully brushed on mascara and lipstick before heading out the door.

Will's office was located in one of the numerous office towers that dominated downtown Chicago. She'd parked in a nearby ramp and walked the block to the building, taking a few moments to rest in the lobby and compose herself.

This was all too strange, she mused. He couldn't really expect her to marry him, could he? This was the twenty-first century and America! Women couldn't be forced into marriage, contract or not. Still, Jane couldn't help but think that marriage to Will McCaffrey could solve a few of her pressing problems— like where she was going to live after she gave up her apartment or how she was going to save enough money to get her business back on stable ground.

"I don't love him," she murmured to herself, letting the words repeat silently in her brain like a mantra. A real marriage, a marriage meant to last, required a level of emotion that Will McCaffrey wasn't capable of returning.

Jane smoothed her skirt again, then started toward the elevator. "Just remain calm and everything will be just fine." After all, she didn't know his motivations in sending her the contract. Maybe this was just his way of convincing her to accept a date.

"That's it," she said, the notion taking hold. Will McCaffrey was a handsome, sexy guy, the kind of guy any woman would want to marry. He'd never be forced to rely on an old contract to get a wife. He could walk down Michigan Avenue with a cardboard sign and come up with ten or fifteen candidates within a single city block. So why was he so determined to go out with her?

The elevator opened on a wide hallway. Directly in front of her, glass doors marked the entrance to the offices of McCaffrey Commercial Properties. A pretty receptionist waited behind a circular desk and smiled as Jane walked through the doors. "Good afternoon," she said. "May I help you?"

"I'm here to see Will McCaffrey," Jane said.

"You must be Miss Singleton." She stepped around the desk. "Mr. McCaffrey asked that I show you to his office. He's in a meeting right now, but he should be through momentarily. Is there anything I can get for you?"

Jane was tempted to ask for a blindfold so she wouldn't have to stare at Will's handsome face, or maybe earplugs so she wouldn't have to listen to his tantalizing voice. Or maybe a bottle of Valium to calm her nerves and quell her racing heart. "No, thank you, I'm fine."

The receptionist led her down a long hall and opened a door at the end of it. "I'll let Mr. McCaffrey know you're here."

"Thanks," Jane said.

After the receptionist walked out, Jane wandered around Will's office, too nervous to sit. His law school diploma was displayed prominently behind his desk and the credenza held a variety of photos, most of them featuring either exotic locales or a golden retriever. What she didn't find was a photo of a wife, or even a girlfriend. Jane ignored the tiny thrill of satisfaction that raced through her. Whether he was involved in a relationship or completely single shouldn't make a difference. She picked up a photo of the dog and stared at it.

"His name is Thurgood."

Jane spun around to find Will standing in the doorway, his shoulder braced against the doorjamb. Her heart stopped for a long moment and she had to gulp down a breath to get it started again. "He's...cute," she murmured.

"He's a big mooch and he sheds all over everything. But I love him. What about you? Do you have any pets?"

Jane shifted uneasily, her feet starting to hurt from the high heels she wore. She wasn't sure what to say. Were they going to waste time with chitchat, or was he planning to explain himself? Will's gaze fixed on her face as he waited for her answer.

With a silent curse, Jane fumbled through her purse and pulled out the copy of the contract. She unfolded it and held it out to him. "You sent this to me."

"Yes, I did," Will said, a smile twitching at the corners of his mouth.

"Why?"

"I thought I made that clear in the letter," he replied.

"You can't be serious." Jane glanced down at contract. "This was just a whim fueled by a fair bit of champagne and whiskey." He'd been drunk and feeling sorry for himself and she'd been caught up in a fantasy that the subject of her silly crush might actually show up in six years, contract in hand.

And now he had. She looked up to see Will sweep a bouquet of roses out from behind his back. "These are for you," he said, grinning, the dimple appearing on his cheek. "English roses. Your favorite, right?"

A shiver skittered down her spine and her indignation wavered. All he'd ever had to do was smile at her and she'd agree to anything from doing his laundry to typing his term papers to helping him pick out gifts for the endless string of girls in his life. Will had always been too charming for his own good—and hers.

But he'd always been a man so completely unattainable that he'd taken on mythic proportions in her mind—the classic profile, a body chiseled by the gods, hands so strong yet sensitive they promised to drive her wild—Jane groaned inwardly. Just a few minutes in his presence and her fantasies were back full force. "It's going to take a lot more than roses and this ridiculous contract to make me marry you."

He took a step toward her, his grin widening. "Then tell me what you want, Janie."

She risked another look at him. Features that had once been almost boyish had taken on a harder edge. He seemed powerful, determined. If he was really bent on marriage, then she was hip-deep in trouble—both legal and emotional. Because when Will McCaffrey wanted something, he usually found a way to get it. She cursed silently at her racing pulse and the flush that warmed her cheeks. "Le-let's suppose for a moment this contract is legal, which I don't think it is. You were drunk and I was...under the influence..." She drew a shaky breath. "Why would you want to marry me anyway? We haven't talked since that day you graduated from law school."

He slowly crossed the room and stood in front of her. The scent of the roses made her head swim and she held her breath, wondering just how much closer he would come, praying he wouldn't touch her.

There had been a time when she'd remembered every single time he'd grabbed her hand or brushed

his shoulder against hers. She'd carried around a cata-
log of such events in her head for years and had taken
pains to forget them all. Will McCaffrey was no longer
the subject of a silly crush or her rampant fantasies. He
was a flesh and blood man, a man who still had the capacity to trample her heart and shred her soul.

"Maybe not," he said. "But that doesn't mean I
haven't thought about you."

"That doesn't count," Jane said. In truth, she'd
thought about him hundreds, maybe even thousands
of times—not in the past six years but just in the past
week since she'd seen him on the street. Her attention
flitted from his startling blue eyes ringed with thick
dark lashes to the tiny dimple in his left cheek, once so
familiar. There was still so much of the college boy left
in him even though the neatly groomed hair and finely
pressed suit made him the picture of respectability.

"Come on, Janie. We were friends once, why can't
we be again? We were good together."

"Did you suffer a head injury recently?" she demanded. "Have you spent time in a psychiatric hospi-
tal? Or are you just seriously delusional? We were
never together. You were together with half the girls
on campus, but never with me."

"You're the only girl—I mean, woman—that I've
ever had a friendship with. And I'm beginning to realize how rare that really is."

He reached out and smoothed his palm along the
length of her arm. She'd watched him charm so many
women, studied his techniques and imagined herself
on the receiving end of his attentions. Well, she wasn't
going to fall for his tricks! "Let's just be honest here."

"Great," Will said. "Now we're getting somewhere. Let's just lay it all out on the table. I'm all for honesty."

"For some reason, you suddenly feel the need to marry me. Maybe you're in the midst of some early midlife crisis. Or maybe you've run through all the single women in the Chicago metro area. Or maybe all your buddies have settled down and you don't have anyone to party with. But rather than dating a woman and going the traditional route, you dug up this contract and wrote me a letter. I suppose you thought I'd jump at the offer. After all, a girl like me would be a fool to turn down an offer of marriage from a guy like you."

He opened his mouth to speak, a frown of confusion furrowing his brow. "What is that supposed to mean?"

"It means I'm not going to marry you! We don't even know each other." She paused. "Anymore. And I don't remember signing this contract." She crumpled it up and shoved it at his chest.

It was a lie. She remembered every moment of that night. She'd been the one to insist they have a witness sign, as well, she'd been the one who'd actually wanted the document to be legal, dreamed that someday he might come back and try to enforce it.

Will drew a deep breath and let it out slowly. "You've changed, Janie. You used to be so..."

"Weak, pathetic, spineless? I'm not that same silly girl who used to hang on your every word, who used to bake you cookies and mend your shirts."

"That's not what I was going to say." He reached out and hesitantly touched her cheek, drawing his thumb over her lower lip. "You're not a girl at all, Janie.

You're a woman. A very beautiful, passionate, stubborn woman."

Jane closed her eyes, losing herself for a moment in the warmth of his hand. Oh, God. This was it. This was the start to one of her top five fantasies! In a few moments, he'd sweep her into his arms and kiss her, ravaging her mouth with his lips. And if by some bizarre shift in the cosmos, her fantasy became reality, then she might as well start shopping for a white dress and a bridal bouquet and those little candy-coated almonds tied up in tulle that always sat on the dinner tables at weddings.

There was no way she was going to avoid falling in love with Will McCaffrey all over again...and right now, with her heart slamming in her chest and her pulse racing, she wasn't even sure she'd ever fallen out of love with him in the first place.

She swallowed hard. "What do you want from me?" she asked, her voice wavering.

"I just want you to forget the past. I want you to go out to dinner with me tonight. I want to share a bottle of champagne and get to know you all over again."

Jane ground her teeth. Why was he so determined to pull her in again? Couldn't he sense what this would cost her? She shook her head. "No. I'm not going to date you and I'm not going to marry you!"

"Why not?" he demanded, frustration coloring his tone. "What's wrong with me? I'm a decent guy. The way you're acting you'd think I was some psychotic ax murderer with a hump on his back and halitosis."

"There's nothing wrong with you. We're just not... suited."

Will chuckled softly, shaking his head. "How can you possibly know that?"

"I just do," Jane replied.

Will shrugged and stepped away from her, the warmth of his touch suddenly going cold. "Then I guess I'll see you in court."

Jane closed her eyes and tried to school her temper. "We have to be able to reach some sort of compromise. If you hadn't run into me on the street the other day, you never would have remembered the contract. And we both would have gone on with our lives."

"Maybe so," he said. "But we did meet again and whether that was destiny or providence, I don't care. It made me realize how much I missed you. And how much I want you in my life again."

Jane forced herself not to dwell on his words. They were all part of his plan to charm her, to suck all the common sense out of her brain so he could have his way with her. "And marriage is the answer? What if I agree to a date? Doesn't that seem a more logical first step?"

"I asked and you said no. Besides, now that I think about it, I'm sick and tired of dating. I'm ready to move on with my life," Will said. He sat down at his desk and leaned back in his chair, linking his fingers behind his head and watching her with a bland smile.

If he wanted a fight, then she was fully prepared to give him one! Jane braced her hands on his desk and leaned over it, meeting his gaze with a glare of her own. "I'm not going to marry you. I'm not going to date you. In fact, I never want to see you again. If you think you can enforce your silly contract, then try it. I dare you."

Her heart pounding, Jane strode to the door and yanked it open. She briefly considered turning around and throwing a few more threats his way, but in the end, she made a quick escape. One more look at Will McCaffrey might be just what it took to push her over the edge, into a strange fantasy world where she really could marry him and live happily-ever-after.

When she reached the elevator, she leaned back against the wall and closed her eyes. Images of Will swam in her head and Jane groaned softly. Fighting him seemed to be the only option. Or was it?

"I just need time," she murmured, her desperation thick in her voice. Time to sort out her financial problems without the threat of an expensive court case hanging over her head. Time to come to grips with her attraction to a man she couldn't possibly love. And time to convince herself that Will McCaffrey wasn't the man of her dreams.

Yet, in a secret corner of her heart, she wondered what might happen if she agreed to marry him. Would he get scared and back down, deftly avoiding commitment as he had in the past? Or would he actually fulfill the terms of their contract and walk down the aisle with her?

Jane groaned softly, her mind spinning with the possibilities. What if she never found out for sure and lived to regret it? The choices she made today might seem like her only option. But how would they look in ten or fifteen years?

2

A CHILLY WIND BLEW OFF the lake, sending dried leaves swirling into the air. The dismal gray sky obscured the November sun and a cold drizzle shone on the sidewalks. Somewhere nearby, a siren wailed. Will drew his overcoat more tightly around him and jogged across the street against the light.

After what had happened at his office two days ago, Will hadn't expected to hear from Jane again. He'd handled their meeting badly, but he'd been thrown off track by the notion that she actually believed he was going to force her to marry him! The contract had only been a means to get her to agree to dinner, but since she'd adamantly refused his invitations, he felt backed into a corner. Will cursed beneath his breath. He'd never had to force a woman to date him before. Why was he so determined to have Jane?

Maybe seeing her again would clarify things in his mind. Yes, she was incredibly attractive, and yes, they had shared a past that included a friendship he'd treasured. But they were different people living different lives now. Did that mean they couldn't begin again? He strolled into the small park across from the Newberry Library and walked along the path, scanning the pedestrians in search of Jane.

She'd left a message for him this morning asking him to meet her, but avoiding any explanation for her request. For now, Will had decided to grab the opportunity to explain his behavior and find a way to set things right with her. At best, she might finally agree to dinner. At worst, she'd tell him exactly where he could shove his contract.

She wasn't the same girl he'd known back in law school. She'd gone from an awkward teenager to a confident woman and for an instant, Will regretted that he hadn't been there to see it—to experience it. Hell, she probably had all the men she needed in her life, men who had recognized her beauty the moment they'd met her, men who'd been a little quicker off the mark than he had been.

Will had been with a lot of women and though the passion had been overwhelming at times, he'd never really connected emotionally, never really believed what they'd shared had anything to do with love or even deep affection. It had always been about physical desire and nothing more.

His feelings for Jane were different. She was incredibly beautiful and sexy and intriguing, but he wasn't intent on seducing her. They were friends first and if they became lovers, it would come as a logical step in their relationship, not from some overwhelming desire to rip each other's clothes off.

Jane wasn't the kind of woman he could seduce and then leave. She occupied a different place in his life than all the other women had. Yet, he couldn't ignore the sparks of attraction that had crackled in the air when they were together these last couple of times.

Nor could he deny spending the last few days thinking about her, about how good it felt to be around her, about how he enjoyed the sound of her voice and warmth of her touch.

What he wanted didn't matter, especially if Jane didn't want him. If she walked up to him and demanded that he stay out of her life, then he'd have no choice but to back off. Will stopped in the middle of the path and cursed softly. He'd always suspected that she'd carried a secret torch for him, that all he'd have had to do was crook his finger and she'd have come willingly. But whatever feelings she might have harbored for him had obviously been forgotten long ago.

He slowly turned and scanned the park again. For an instant, he thought he saw her sitting on a bench on the far side, but then he realized it wasn't her. He sat down to wait, watching an elderly man toss a tennis ball to his terrier. After ten minutes, Will began to wonder if he'd been stood up, but then he saw her striding briskly toward him. He stood and she stopped short, watching him for a long moment.

They slowly approached each other, their gazes locked, meeting in the center of the square. "I thought you might have decided not to come," he said when she stood in front of him.

"I almost didn't," Jane replied.

A long silence grew between them and Will fought the urge to reach out and brush a windblown strand of hair out of her eyes. If he could just touch her, then everything would be all right. But he shoved his hands into his coat pockets to ward off temptation. "Would you like to go somewhere, maybe get a cup of coffee? There's a place just down the—"

Jane shook her head. "No, this will be fine right here. I just have one question to ask and I want you to be completely honest with me."

"All right," Will said.

"Why are you doing this? You could have any woman you wanted. Why me?"

"That's two questions," he said. "With very different answers."

"Tell me," Jane insisted. "The truth."

Will carefully considered his answer, knowing what he said might make all the difference in her decision. He was tempted to lie, to cover up his real motivations. But if this was going to work, he couldn't begin with a lie. "I'm thirty years old. My father has been pressuring me to get serious about my future. To find a wife and to start a family. But my social life up until now hasn't really been focused on that particular goal. I thought I might try another approach. If I want to run his company, I need to show him I'm serious about finding a wife."

Will decided to stop there. The rest was too difficult to explain. It wasn't as if he was using her for his own professional gains, though he knew his father would probably consider Jane a perfect catch for a wife. But whether his job was at stake or not, Will still wanted to be with Jane. And looking into her eyes, he had to wonder if there was something more between them, something he couldn't quite explain.

He waited for Jane's reaction, waited for her to tear into him or to walk away in disgust or start crying uncontrollably. But all she did was nod. "All right, I can understand that. And why me?"

He shrugged. "It makes sense, Janie. First, there's the contract. And we were good friends." He stopped again before revealing the rest of the truth—he was genuinely attracted to Jane, almost overwhelmingly attracted to her. Since they'd met that day on the street outside her office, he'd been plagued with thoughts of her. He was seeing Jane in a whole new light—as a beautiful, intriguing, sexy woman.

"So this is all just a matter of...efficiency?" she asked.

Will chuckled softly. "I've spent years perfecting my considerable charm, but where has it gotten me? I still haven't found the perfect woman."

"So you're willing to settle for the imperfect?"

"No!" Will protested. "You're not imperfect, not at all. We began as friends, Janie. Maybe that's the way it should be." He paused. "If you want my opinion, I think we've all been sold a bill of goods. We're out there looking for love and romance and happily-ever-afters, but for most of us, those things just aren't in the cards and they may never be. I'm thirty years old. I've dated enough to know that finding something special is difficult at best." He closed his eyes and took a deep breath of the damp air. "Would it be so bad just to try? What do either of us have to lose?"

He stared down at her, watching her emotions shift across her face like sunlight on water. She was wavering and Will fought the urge to push her just a little bit closer to the edge. All he needed was one night, one perfect date to get her to see that he was right about them.

"We're different people. You don't know me anymore."

He stared down into her gaze. "I know enough," he said. "I know we'd be good together. Give me a chance to prove it to you."

She gnawed at her lower lip as she considered his offer and Will allowed himself to feel a small measure of hope. "All right," she finally said. "But it has to be on my terms."

"We can do that." He reached out to grab her hands, but she avoided his touch, clutching her fingers in front of her. "Any terms are good with me."

She met his gaze and for a moment, he thought he saw a hint of defiance there. "I want a ring. A really big ring. At least three carats."

Will caught the gasp of surprise before it left his throat. "What?"

"And I don't want to waste time on a long engagement. If it doesn't work after three months, we go our separate ways and we'll tear up the contract. Of course, I get to keep the ring. Agreed?"

She wasn't talking about a dinner date anymore! She was still stuck on the notion that he'd enforce their contract and she'd moved on to something much more serious. His brain scrambled to make sense of it all. Ring? Engagement? Will tried to think rationally, then slowly realized what he'd seen in her eyes. She was calling his bluff—trying to scare him off with the prospect of commitment. Trying to render his contract null and void.

He bit back a chuckle at her audacity. Two could play at this game.

"All right," he said in a measured tone. "But I have some terms of my own. If we're going to give this a real shot, then we have to spend more time together. Quality time. I think you should move in with me. That will give us a chance to see if we're really compatible."

She stiffened slightly and Will knew that he'd put her on the ropes. She'd back down now.

Jane shrugged. "I suppose that would be all right, with one condition. We would have separate bedrooms."

God, she was good. She hadn't even blinked an eye. They'd gone from dating to living together to discussing sleeping arrangements in the course of a minute. "All right, but you'll have to at least make an effort to perform some wifely duties." That was bound to send her over the edge, Will mused. Play the male chauvinist card and he'd be back on top again.

As expected, Jane's composure cracked and her eyes suddenly went wide. "You want me to have sex with you?"

Will laughed. "No, that's not what I meant. But if you'd like to add that to your list of daily responsibilities, I wouldn't object."

"This is not going to work," she muttered.

"I was talking about things that wives generally do for their husbands. Cook a meal every now and then, do a little laundry, make a comfortable home, listen to my problems about work."

"And what about a husband's duties? What are you going to contribute to this arrangement?"

"Whatever you need. Whatever you want. You name it and it's yours."

"A lock on my bedroom door," she muttered. "And my own bathroom."

"Well, that's going to be a problem," he said. "My house only has one. And a half."

She sighed, regarding him with a suspicious glare. "I suppose I could deal with that. We can work out a schedule for the bathroom."

"Agreed," he said.

"All right. Three months," she said. "Until Valentine's Day. And if it doesn't work, we'll go our separate ways."

"Three months," he said. "Who knows what might happen?"

She held out her hand. At first he wasn't sure what she meant to do and he reached out to take her fingers in his. But she gave his hand a firm shake. "It's a deal. Maybe we should write up another contract."

Still stunned by the sudden turn of events, Will could only press her hand between his, unwilling to let her go. "We'll just make an addendum to the old contract," he said. "So when would you like to move in?"

"This weekend?" she asked.

"All right." He couldn't resist a smile. "How about Saturday? We'll get you all settled and then maybe we can go out and have some dinner. I know this great restaurant on—"

"I have to work on Saturday, so Sunday would be better."

"2234 North Winston in DePaul. I'll expect you Sunday."

She nodded, then turned to walk away. But he stopped her, refusing to let go of her hand. "Jane?"

She stared down at their fingers, now entwined. "Yes?"

"You asked me why. I could ask you the same question. Why?"

"I don't have to give you my reasons," she said. "That's not part of the deal." With that, she tugged out of his grasp and strode down the sidewalk. He watched her until she turned a corner and disappeared. Then Will slowly sank down on a nearby park bench, his breath clouding in front of his face.

From the start, all he'd really wanted was a date. And now, he suddenly had a fiancée! He wasn't quite sure what to think. In the end, he decided to put off thinking about Jane Singleton at all. He'd have three months to figure out how he really felt about her—and how she felt about him.

CARDBOARD BOXES CLUTTERED the floor in Jane's bedroom. She stared at the summer side of her closet, wondering what to do with the simple cotton dresses and lightweight tops hanging there. "I'll put these in storage," she murmured.

Lisa sat on the edge of the bed, sipping a Starbucks latte and watching as Jane moved around the room, tossing clothing and toiletries into various boxes.

"You're crazy. What has gotten into you, Jane?" She held up her hand to stop Jane's response. "Wait, don't answer that. I know exactly what's gotten into you. An insidious little virus called Will McCaffrey. And here, I thought you'd finally been cured."

"What has gotten into me is a good case of common sense," Jane said, grabbing a stack of neatly folded sweaters and placing them into an empty box.

She'd spent two nights tossing and turning, considering all her options. But in the end, it hadn't been the tossing and turning that had forced her hand. Instead it had been the phone call from her auto mechanic, informing her that she'd have to replace the transmission on her nine-year-old car, a repair that she didn't have the money to pay for—especially if she had to pay some downtown lawyer to get her out of Will's ridiculous contract.

"Common sense?" Lisa squawked. "How could moving in with Will McCaffrey have anything to do with common sense?"

"I'm not just moving in with him. I'm kind of...engaged."

Lisa's mouth dropped open in astonishment. "Kind of?"

Jane turned her attention back to the stack of sweaters she needed to pack. "I thought I could force him to give up on his stupid contract. I thought once he was faced with the realities of commitment, he'd back off right away and I'd be free of him. It just didn't work out as I planned."

"Jane, I can't believe that contract would hold up. He can't force you to marry him."

"That's not the point. It's going to cost me to fight him either way, money I don't have. Besides, this will work out just fine. I'll have a place to live while I get back on my feet, and after three months, we'll tear up the contract and I'll never have to think about Will

McCaffrey again." She paused in her packing and turned to her friend. "I can do this, Lisa. It's only three months. We'll put an effort into the business, make enough money to get us through the winter, and in March, we'll start over again."

"I told you, you could come and stay with me and Roy. Our sofa is really comfortable."

"No, I couldn't."

"You haven't even considered your parents."

"The drive back and forth between Lake Geneva and the city would be too much of a grind. And I can't tell my mother about our business problems. She's always wanted me to give up my career and find a husband, ever since we started Windy City Gardens. If she knew the business was this close to folding, she'd have every unmarried doctor in the Chicago metro area lined up at my front door."

"There has to be another solution."

"What choice do I have? If I move in with him, that will buy me some time."

"Janie, I hate to state the obvious here, but this is not a guy you should live with. You know how long it took to get over your infatuation with him. Are you willing to jump back into that fire all over again?"

"I'm a different person now. I see him for what he really is."

"And what is that? An incredibly handsome, sexy, successful man." Lisa clapped her palms to her cheeks in mock horror. "Oh, my God, I can see why you'd be repelled. What a nightmare!"

Jane smiled at her friend's silly expression. "Yes, he's sexy, but it's not like I can't resist."

"You never could," Lisa said. "But let's be honest, Jane. Will McCaffrey always made you feel second best. While he was off romancing his latest conquest, you just waited for whatever crumbs he'd throw your way, certain he was your Prince Charming. It was only after he disappeared from your life that you really began to come into your own. And that says more about him than it does about you, don't you think?"

Jane sighed softly, the truth of her friend's words cutting deep. Every instinct told her that being close to Will *was* dangerous. But she still felt the need to prove she wasn't the same girl she'd been six years ago. Nor was she the same girl her mother had raised, sheltering her and protecting her from anything that wasn't clean and pretty and safe, putting silly notions into her head about love and romance and marriage. She'd been naive and far too idealistic when she'd first met Will. Was it any wonder she'd created an elaborate fantasy world around a man who'd treated her like a little sister?

But she was a woman now and Jane knew things had changed. Whatever brotherly thoughts Will may have had all those years ago were long gone. She saw it in the way he looked at her. There was more there than just friendship and she wanted to know exactly what it was. "I'm not that silly girl anymore," Jane murmured.

"And he's not that cute law student who lives downstairs. Picture this. You wake up in the morning and wander into the bathroom, only to find him stepping out of the shower, dripping wet and wearing only his birthday suit. Or you get up late at night for a glass of water and he's there, asleep on the sofa in his boxer shorts, his chest all bare and gleaming in the light from the television. Yes, you have grown up. You're a woman and he's a man, a man who is full-blown fantasy material. And don't tell me you haven't imagined him stark naked and...aroused. And lying in a bed just a few feet away." Lisa pressed her hand to her heart and sighed. "Proximity can destroy even the strongest resolve."

"But I have a plan," Jane said.

"What? You're going to wear a blindfold and a chastity belt for the next three months?"

"No. I'm going to throw myself into the wife role and prove to him that I'm the last person he'd want to marry. I might not even need a lawyer. After three months, he'll be ready to show me the door."

Lisa groaned and covered her face with her hands. "That's not going to work. I know you, Janie, and you'd make a really good wife." She flopped back on the bed and stared at the ceiling. "You cook and you bake and you're a pretty decent decorator. You even know how to make curtains. I have no doubt you could throw a dinner party for twelve with just twenty-four hours notice."

"See, all that time my mother spent training me for my eventual place as wife and mother hasn't gone to waste," Jane teased. She crawled onto the bed and crossed her legs in front of her. "I do know how to be the perfect wife. But in knowing that, I also know how to be an imperfect wife. A nagging, horrible, shrew of a wife who can't cook or clean and who thinks hot pink is the height of fashion for interior decor."

"What?" Lisa frowned but then realization slowly

dawned. "Oh." She grinned as she sat up. "Oh, now, that *is* a plan!"

Jane grinned. "I know. It's brilliant in its simplicity, isn't it?"

"Make the man miserable and he'll have no choice but to cut you loose. Jane Singleton, I didn't realize you had such a devious streak."

"He thinks he knows me, but he doesn't. Not anymore. I'm not Plain Jane Singleton anymore. I'm going to be the fiancée from hell, the woman who makes his life miserable. Do you want to place any bets on how long he keeps me around?"

Lisa's smile faded slightly. "That's not what I'm worried about," she said. "I'm worried that once you see what life is like with Will McCaffrey, you're not going to want to leave."

WILL PACED BACK AND FORTH in front of the door, his hands shoved into his pockets, his gaze fixed on the floor. Waiting for Jane to arrive had turned into agony. To pass the time, Will had decided to clean the house, but occupying his hands with dirty dishes and dusting hadn't helped calm his nerves. He found himself waiting for the phone to ring, anticipating a call from Jane saying she'd changed her mind.

Had anyone told him a few weeks ago that he'd be in this position, waiting for a woman to move into his house, he'd have laughed. Living with a woman would seriously cramp his lifestyle, never mind accepting the prospect of being with the same person day after day.

But he found himself looking forward to having Jane close by. He remembered all the conversations they'd had in the past, how much fun it was to talk to her, how he appreciated her thoughtful responses and level-headed advice. And her temperament was well suited to him—she spoke her mind without getting emotional, like women tended to do.

Still, arguing with Jane might actually be fun, Will mused. He'd seen flashes of a temper over the past few days, proving that a very determined woman had replaced the passive girl he'd once known. She was stubborn and opinionated and...passionate.

Passionate and very beautiful. Will couldn't ignore that particular benefit, either. He'd never get tired of looking at Jane. Her beauty wasn't painted on or surgically enhanced or chemically altered. When he looked at her, Will knew he was looking at a real woman. Her beauty was simple, artless, so natural that he knew it would become more striking with every passing day.

Will was standing in front of the door when the security buzzer rang. Thurgood jumped up from the living-room sofa where he'd been sleeping and began to bark. "Quiet," Will said, wiping his sweaty palms on his T-shirt. He took a deep breath. "And be nice to the lady. No jumping, no drooling, no licking. And keep your nose out of her...well, you know. No sniffing." He'd do well to follow his own advice, Will thought, chuckling softly.

Will paused before he opened the door. He'd expected this moment would be accompanied by a fair amount of dread. After all, he had the perfect bachelor pad, comfortable, functional, chintz-free. No doubt she'd expect to make a few changes. "We draw the line at pink," Will said to Thurgood. "If she brings anything pink into this house, I'm going to have to lodge a formal protest and you're going to gnaw it to shreds."

The house had everything a guy could want—flat screen television, a killer stereo system, a nice weight machine and not one, but two leather recliners. Will winced. So maybe it wasn't a bastion of femininity, but he was ready to add a few women's touches—a few fancy dish towels, maybe some curtains, a couple of throw pillows. "I can be flexible, I can compromise."

Thurgood sat in front of the door, his tail thumping on the hardwood floor. Even if this didn't work out, it would be a good experience. Maybe he'd learn a little bit more about women, knowledge that would help him find a wife. And, if it did work out, then making a few changes in his life was a small price to pay to find a woman to love.

Will sighed. Was he being too optimistic, thinking that he and Jane had a chance? They respected each other as friends. And he had to admit that there had been times when he preferred to spend a chaste afternoon with Jane rather that a hot night in bed with any other woman. Will hoped that, given time, they could recapture that closeness.

The bell rang again and Will quickly opened the front door. Jane stood behind a potted palm, her face obscured. He quickly grabbed the plant from her arms and stepped back. "Come on in," he said.

Will set the palm down on the floor and glanced up at her. His breath caught in his throat. Though she was dressed casually in jeans and a sweater, and her hair was tied back with a scarf, she still looked incredibly beautiful. He couldn't get over how much she'd changed, yet how much she still looked like the fresh-faced nineteen-year-old girl he'd known.

Jane hesitated for a moment before stepping inside, as if she were still wavering on her decision. Thurgood wriggled in front of her and she eyed him warily. But then she moved forward and Will breathed a silent sigh of relief. "I'll show you around," he said. "This is Thurgood. He's a golden retriever"

"He's big," Jane murmured. "Really...big."

"You don't like dogs? Didn't you ever have a dog when you were a kid?"

"My mother didn't like animals. Too messy. I had plants for pets." She forced a smile and pointed to the palm. "Maybe I should get the rest of my things," she said, making for the door. "Regina is a little sensitive to the cold. I wrapped Anya in plastic, but she's probably going to suffer from shock anyway."

"Regina? Anya?"

"Don't you remember them? Regina is a *sedum morganianum* and Anya is a *pellaea rotundifolia*. More commonly known as a burro tail and a button fern."

He reached out and caught her hand and held tight. "Still naming your plants."

"Still the same plants," she said hurrying out the door.

Will trailed after her, jogging down the front steps to the street. "I'll help you. Lifting and toting is a husband's responsibility."

"Are you saying I can't carry my own things?" she asked, a hint of defensiveness in her voice.

"Nope. I was just saying I'd be happy to do it for you."

"All right then," Jane said. "But I don't want you to think I'm incapable of carrying a few plants and some heavy boxes."

Will grinned, stepping around her to stop her retreat. She bumped into him and he grabbed her waist. "I think you're probably capable of doing anything you set your mind to." For an instant, he thought about pulling her closer and kissing her, just to break the tension between them. But Will didn't want to frighten her off before she even moved in. He had three months to discover what Jane felt like and tasted like. He could be patient.

"Well, we'd better get busy," she murmured.

Will nodded. She'd packed her plants and boxes in the back of a pickup truck, emblazoned with the Windy City Gardens logo, which she'd double-parked in front of the house. Will quickly helped her unload the truck, carrying her things up the front steps and leaving them just inside the front door. When they'd finished, he sent her inside, then hopped in her truck, drove it around to the alley and parked it in his garage.

When he got back into the house, he found Jane in the kitchen, watering a plant that looked a bit wilted. "Is it going to be all right?"

She jumped slightly, as if he'd surprised her, then turned around. "I think so. It isn't a very good time of year to be moving plants. Plants get used to their environment and sometimes they get a little...upset if you alter their living conditions."

He stepped up behind her and stared at the plant, a memory niggling at his brain. "Who is this?"

"Sabrina. Don't you remember her?"

"From college?" Will asked.

Jane nodded. "You gave her to me after I typed that article for law review. She's old, but she's still very healthy. Philodendrons aren't susceptible to bugs or disease and I've repotted her a couple of times."

"And you named her Sabrina because..."

"Audrey Hepburn. Humphrey Bogart."

"Right. That movie." He backed away, certain if he didn't, he'd bend closer and kiss the curve of her neck. His gaze fixed on the spot just beneath her ear and wondered if he pressed his lips to her skin, if she'd taste as good as she smelled. He drew a breath and tried to place the scent. It wasn't heavy or intense, but barely perceptible, like the hint of flowers on a summer breeze. Will drew another breath, then pasted a smile on his face. No sniffing! "I guess I should show you around."

Jane turned to face him. "All right."

As he led her through the house, Jane carefully examined her new surroundings with curiosity. And Will used the opportunity to touch her again and again, resting his palm at the small of her back, grasping her elbow as he steered her from room to room. Thurgood followed behind them, anxious to figure out this new visitor.

"I bought the house because of the high ceilings," Will explained. "And the architectural details. The crown mouldings are original and so is the mantel in the living room. When I bought the place, they were covered with layers of paint."

She nodded. "It's beautiful. But the decor is so modern."

"Yeah, I like that clean look. Steel and glass and leather."

"Very manly," Jane murmured.

"I'll show you your bedroom," he said, pulling her along to the stairs, lacing his fingers through hers. "You saw the kitchen and the family room in the back. There are three bedrooms and a bath upstairs. The third floor is one big, unfinished room. I'm not sure what I'm going to do with that space yet."

When they got to the top of the stairs, he pointed into the smallest of the rooms. "I use that as an office. And this is my room." He pushed the door open to reveal a large bed with a simple Danish style dresser and wardrobe.

Will stepped across the hall and opened the door to the smaller guest room. "And this is your room. It's not much, but I'm sure you'll have some things of your own to make it look prettier."

She stepped into the room then quickly spun around, running into him as she tried to leave. "I don't think this is a good idea. I—I'm sorry. I think I'm just going to go."

Will gently grabbed her arms to halt her escape. "You don't have anything to fear from me, Janie," he murmured, staring down at her beautiful face. He hooked his finger under her chin, forcing her gaze to meet his. "You're safe here. I swear you are."

"I—I know," she murmured, her words as doubtful as the look on her face.

"Give this a chance to work." He bent closer, his gaze fixed on her lips. Every instinct told him not to kiss her—it was too soon, she was too skittish. When she drew in a sharp breath, the sound penetrated his hazy thoughts and Will froze, halfway to her mouth. Reluctantly he met her eyes, seeing the doubt and apprehension there, and he knew he'd made a mistake. "Sorry," he murmured. "I—we shouldn't—I'm just going to go get your things from downstairs, okay?"

She nodded slowly. "Okay."

Will jogged down the stairs. But he walked right by the boxes and plants and headed to the kitchen. When he reached the sink, he turned on the cold water and rubbed his wet hands over his face. With a soft curse, he grabbed a kitchen towel and leaned back against the edge of the counter, his eyes closed, his face dripping.

A few seconds later, Thurgood trotted into the kitchen and sat down next to the sink. "What do you think?" Will asked. "I know, I know, she's a girl. But she's really pretty, don't you think?"

Thurgood tilted his head, cocking an ear up, as if he didn't approve of their new houseguest.

Will reached down and patted the dog on the head. "She'll just take a little getting used to." He tossed the towel on the counter and headed back to the stairs, stacking three boxes and carrying them to her bedroom.

Will found her sitting on the edge of the bed, her hands clutching Regina or Anya, he couldn't remember which. She looked like she was about ready to cry

and Will quickly set down the boxes and knelt in front
of her. "What's wrong?"

Jane forced a smile and shook her head. "Nothing."

"Come on, what?"

She glanced around. "This doesn't feel like home."

Suddenly the confident, determined woman was
gone, replaced by the girl he'd known, the girl who
cried at the end of romantic movies, the girl who wore
her heart on her sleeve. If this arrangement was making her so miserable, then why had she agreed to it?
Will searched her face for answers, but found none. He
suddenly felt as if he'd forced her into something she
didn't want.

He cursed himself and tried to think of a way to
make her smile again. He usually knew exactly how to
please a woman, but Jane Singleton had a way of
throwing him off balance. She seemed immune to his
tried and true tricks. And his charm didn't seem to
work on her, either. "Well, you have to fix it up. Buy
some...curtains or pictures or whatever. I could get
you a flat screen television if you want. You could
watch your old movies in here." That brought a smile
and Will breathed a silent sigh of relief that no tears
were shed.

"I think I *will* do a little redecorating," she said.

"Go for it. Hell, you can paint the house pink for all I
care." Will stood, grabbing her hands as he did. "Why
don't I finish bringing up your boxes and plants and
then we'll go out and get some dinner?"

"Isn't one of my wifely duties to make you dinner?"
Jane asked.

"Yes. And one of my husbandly duties is to treat you

to a night out. I'm afraid all I have in the kitchen is peanut butter, bread, milk and beer. I don't expect you to cook with that."

"I *am* hungry."

Will smiled and tugged her along to the door. He knew the first night was going to be difficult, but he'd do his best to make her feel comfortable. He'd buy her dinner, he'd soothe her fears and he'd do his best to keep from kissing her every time he looked at her.

3

THE HOUSE WAS DARK as Jane and Will walked up the front steps. Will unlocked the door, then walked inside and turned off the security system. Thurgood was waiting, sitting patiently nearby. The dog watched Jane with a wary eye and she gave him a wide berth as she walked inside.

She wasn't sure she trusted the animal. Her mother had been pathological when it came to housecleaning and a shedding pet was out of the question. So as a child, Jane had turned to plants. Her first "pet" had been an African violet that had died when she'd misted it with cheap perfume. Though plants weren't a great substitute for a puppy or a kitten, she'd been forced to make do. And that odd little part of her childhood had led her to her career.

Will helped her out of her jacket, then hung it up in the hall closet. She stared at the jacket, tucked in among his coats and thought how strange it was. She had a roommate, a roommate who'd spent the evening charming her with silly stories about his work and his travels. A roommate who had the bluest eyes she'd ever seen and the warmest laugh she'd ever heard. And a roommate who took advantage of every opportunity to touch her, to smooth his hand across her back or twist his fingers through hers. At first, his touch had disarmed her, sending her heart into overdrive. But during the course of the evening, she'd found his touch soothing, comforting, allaying her apprehensions and insecurities.

"I forgot to give this to you," Will said.

Jane glanced up and hesitantly reached out to take a key from him, her fingers brushing against his. "What is this for?"

"For the front door. Actually, for all the doors. You're going to need one now that you're living here."

"Oh, right," she said, slipping the key into her pocket.

Jane had anticipated all the difficulties involved in occupying the same space as Will and she'd steeled herself for a long adjustment period. But she'd been surprised at how easily they'd slipped back into familiar patterns, Jane listening raptly while Will entertained her, Will making her feel like the most fascinating woman on the planet. It wasn't hard to see why she'd fallen madly in love with him all those years ago—and why she'd had such a hard time forgetting him.

"And the security code is 2-2-3-3," he added. "When you open the door or leave, just punch in those numbers and hit the Set button."

"Fine," she murmured, stepping forward and staring at the keypad.

He reached over her shoulder to point to the correct button and his arm brushed against her body, sending a current through her limbs. She held her breath and tried to quiet her racing pulse, but it was no use. Just having him so near was enough to rattle her resolve. Even now, as he stood just behind her, Jane realized how much she craved the sensation of his hands on her skin, the warmth of his shoulder pressed against hers, the soft tickle of his breath in her hair.

She closed her eyes and waited, saying a silent prayer that she'd be able to keep her wits about her, yet secretly hoping he'd at least try to test her limits. She felt as if she were teetering on the edge of a deep, dark abyss, barely able to keep her balance, knowing that danger waited below. Had she been more experienced with men, she might have just taken the leap and ignored the danger. What did she have to lose—besides her heart?

"It's been a long day," she murmured.

"You must be tired," he said, his voice soft in her ear.

She slowly turned, but he didn't move away. Instead he held his ground, trapping her between the door and his body. Her gaze fixed on his chest and she was afraid to look up, afraid she'd see desire in his eyes and not know what to do. The anticipation was acute as she tried to guess what was going through his mind. She was a woman, he was a man, they were alone and his bedroom was just a few steps away.

He probably assumed it would be simple to seduce her. He'd begin by kissing her, softly at first and then more intensely. And then, his hands would wander over her body, touching her provocatively, exploring sensitive spots with his fingers and then with his mouth. After that, the clothes would go and passion would overwhelm common sense. They'd tumble into bed and she'd be lost forever.

With a silent curse, Jane stepped away from him. She couldn't succumb—not now, not ever! This was a temporary arrangement at best and when she walked away in a few months, she wouldn't be dragging a big old torch behind her. "I'm going to go to bed."

"I—I guess I'll see you in the morning," Will said, as if startled by her abrupt words. "Is there anything I can get for you?"

Jane shook her head. "No, I'm fine. Thank you for dinner, Will."

"It was fun," Will said. "I'd forgotten how easy it is to talk to you."

She felt a blush warm her cheeks as she headed for the stairs. When she reached the safety of her bedroom, she quickly closed the door and leaned back against it. Jane glanced at her watch and was surprised to see that it was nearly midnight. She and Lisa had a job lined up for the next day and were due on site at daybreak. Even if she fell asleep this minute, she'd only get five hours. And the way Jane felt, she knew sleep wouldn't come easily.

She tugged her sweater over her head and tossed it on a nearby chair, then slowly stripped out of the rest of her clothes. When she was wrapped in her robe, Jane crossed the room to the bed and sat down.

"What are we doing here, Anya?" she murmured as she picked up the button fern from the bedside table. "Maybe we should have gone to live with Mom and Dad. The commute would have been a lot easier to take than this." Jane grabbed a misting bottle and sprayed the fern before she set Anya back in her spot. "I thought I had a plan. But whenever he touches me, all my romantic circuits just go...haywire. You know what I mean?"

Jane stared at the plant for a long moment. "Of course you don't know what I mean. You're a plant. You don't even know what sex is." She took a ragged breath. "Lucky fern."

That was exactly her problem, Jane mused. She knew all about sex, all about what could happen between a man and a woman, what *should* happen, especially with a man as skilled in seduction as Will was. What she hadn't experienced firsthand with the handful of lovers that she'd had, she'd read about in books and magazines. And with all the knowledge she'd gathered, Jane had come to one uncomfortable conclusion—she'd never really had great sex. She probably hadn't even had good sex. Nope, she was sure what she'd experienced had barely risen to the level of mediocre.

She'd just always been so nervous and hesitant, certain her inexperience would show. Enjoyment had always been secondary to just getting through the event without making any major gaffes. Sex had to be better than what she'd encountered in the past. If it wasn't, then why did humans spend so much time thinking about it and talking about—and doing it?

With a soft groan, Jane flopped back on the bed and stared at the ceiling. Unbidden images drifted through her mind, naked bodies, rumpled sheets, tangled limbs. She pinched her eyes shut and tried to think about something less dangerous. "Maidenhair fern: *Adiantum capillus-veneris*. Ostrich fern: *Matteuccia stru-*

thiopteris. Cinnamon fern: *Osmunda cinnamomea.* Royal fern: *Osmunda regalis.''*

Reciting botanical names had always calmed her mind. Sometimes she used ferns, sometimes common weeds. When she really couldn't sleep, she'd start on trees or garden vegetables. Herbs usually worked in the wee hours of the morning. But as she rattled off another list of ferns, Jane realized that her efforts would be futile. Sooner or later, she'd have to stop and then the thoughts would come back.

''Maple trees: *Acer.* Sugar maple: *Acer saccharum.* Paperbark maple: *Acer griseum.* Norway maple: *Acer platanoides.''*

By the time she'd run through deciduous and coniferous trees, the house had gone silent. Jane rolled off the bed and tiptoed to the door, then carefully pulled it open. She held her breath and listened, but the only sounds she heard were outside the house—traffic, a siren, the hum of the city.

Will had left the bathroom light on and she made her way down the hall. A hot shower would probably help her sleep. Or maybe a bubble bath. But before she reached the bathroom, she had to pass Will's room. Jane hesitated when she saw the door was slightly ajar. Her curiosity overcame her nerves and she craned her neck to see inside.

Her breath caught in her throat as she watched him, the light from the hall just barely illuminating his form. Sprawled on his bed, he lay with one arm above his head, the other hanging off the side. His chest was bare and the sheet bunched around his waist, leaving one leg exposed. Jane knew he was naked beneath the sheet. She also knew staring at him wasn't doing her any good.

But he was so beautiful, devilishly handsome and undeniably sexy. She wondered what would happen if she walked into his room, shrugged out of her robe and crawled into bed with him. Would he be startled to find her there or would he accept her presence as if it were inevitable?

Maybe she ought to reconsider her scheme. She could always spend the next three months in bed with Will, enjoying all the pleasures of the flesh—his flesh. She could say it was part of her duties as his fiancée and future wife. Laundry and grocery shopping. Hot, sweaty sex and earth-shattering orgasms.

Jane swallowed hard and backed away from the door. "Birch trees," she murmured, "Fraxinus. No, Fagus." She drew a ragged breath and walked to the bathroom. "Birch trees: *Betula*. Paper birch: *Betula papyrifera*." A shiver skittered through her. "Dark hair and long legs. Smooth skin and hard muscle. Eyes so blue it aches to look at them."

Whether she chose trees or body parts, nothing in the world would put her to sleep tonight—not with Will McCaffrey lying in the next room, warm and naked and willing to please.

"WHAT IS THAT SMELL? It smells like something died in here."

"That's dinner," Jane said. She turned to smile at Lisa as her friend followed her into Will's kitchen. Thurgood trotted after them, resuming his place in front of the refrigerator. "Liver and onions. It's all part of my diabolical plan to render this silly contract null and void." She stopped at the fancy commercial-style stove and pulled up the lid of the frying pan. "Yummy."

Lisa wrinkled her nose. "Your first dinner with Will and you're feeding him that?"

"It's time to separate the men from the boys, the real husband material from the pretenders. If he really wants to marry me, then he'll eat this with a smile. If he doesn't, then I'm well on my way to tearing up that contract."

"And what if he really does want to marry you? What if he eats the liver and asks for seconds."

"He won't. I know Will McCaffrey and he's not the marrying type." Jane quickly replaced the lid on the pan. "Did you find an apron?"

Lisa held up the bag. "Do you know how many places I had to look? They don't sell aprons anymore. I borrowed this from my Nana Harper." She yanked a gingham-checked version from the paper bag and handed it to Jane.

"Oh, it's got a ruffle. This is perfect," she said as she tied it around her waist.

"You look like June Cleaver," Lisa muttered. "All you need now is the pearls."

"I have pearls," Jane said. "I'll just—"

"Don't you think you're taking this a little too far?" Lisa asked. "It's obvious you like this guy. It seems as if he likes you. Why not just forget all this scheming and see what happens?"

"I can't do that." Though the notion was tempting, Jane knew far too well the power that Will McCaffrey held over her. If she admitted she felt even a shred of attraction to him, then she was lost. She'd fall hopelessly in love with him and he'd be charming and attentive and wonderful—until someone more interesting and more beautiful came along.

Jane leaned against the counter and drew a deep breath. "Don't you understand what's happening here? He thinks I'm the same old Janie Singleton, shy and silly and stupid, the kind of girl who'd jump at the chance to be with him. The kind of girl I was all those years back when I thought he'd hung the moon and stars. And that's fine, because if he underestimates me, then I've got the advantage."

"But you still want him, don't you?"

Jane glanced over at Lisa and sighed in frustration. "No! Don't be silly, I—"

"You still want him," Lisa said, this time taking the question out of her voice.

"I can't want him. If I do, he'll hurt me. He'll love me for a while, he'll treat me like I'm the most beautiful, interesting woman in the world and then one day, he'll realize I'm not. And he'll move on."

"Unless he wants to marry you," Lisa said.

"He doesn't. It's all just an act," Jane explained, grabbing up a knife and slicing cucumbers for the salad. "Will wants to take over the family business, his father wants him to get married and Will thinks if he shows his father he can be serious about commitment, his father will give him what he wants. But I'll prove to you that Will's not really serious. At the first sign of trouble he'll balk. All I have to do is be clingy or needy or naggy and he'll decide that marriage to me would be more like a prison sentence than a lifelong love affair."

"But that's not who you are," Lisa said, reaching out to pat Jane on the shoulder. "You're smart and funny and any man would be lucky to have you as a wife."

"What about David? I've dated him for over a year and we've never moved past a peck on the cheek."

"David is gay," Lisa insisted.

Jane groaned and buried her face in her hands. "He is, isn't he. I kept hoping he was just sensitive or maybe a little shy with women. I kept telling myself I wanted a man who didn't always think about sex, sex, sex. But he never thinks about sex—at least not with me."

"What are you going to do about David?"

"I guess I don't need to do anything about him. He's gay."

"Yes, he is." Lisa smiled. "And what about Will?"

"Oh, he's definitely not gay. Not by a long shot. And I'm pretty sure he thinks about sex all the time. I'm not sure he can look at a woman and not think about sex. Except maybe when he looks at me."

Lisa sat down on one of the stools at the edge of the granite-covered island. "And when you look at him? How do *you* feel?"

"When he smiles I get this fluttery feeling in my stomach. And last night, he was telling this silly joke and all of a sudden, I couldn't breathe. And then I saw him naked in bed and—"

"What?" Lisa screeched, leaning forward over the counter.

"Last night. I got up and I—I peeked in his bedroom.

And he was sleeping...in his bed...and I think he was naked."

"Was he or wasn't he naked?"

"Well, from the waist up and from the thighs down he was. I'm not sure what was going on beneath the sheets."

"But you wanted to find out, right?"

"No!" Jane reached out and gave Lisa a playful slap. A giggle slipped from her lips. "No. The one time he kissed me I almost fainted. Good grief, if I ever saw him naked I'd probably have a stroke."

"That kiss was six years ago," Lisa muttered, sitting back down. "Don't you think it's time to update that little experience? Why live with an old memory when you can have the real thing?"

"I can't just kiss him," Jane said.

Lisa cupped her chin in her hand. "Why not? Just plant a big wet one on his lips and see what he does. If this is all just an act, then he won't kiss you back. And if it isn't, then we have something new and exciting to discuss."

Jane smoothed her hands over her apron. "I don't think June Cleaver—or my mother—would approve of such an aggressive move."

Lisa groaned and rolled her eyes. "I give up. I'm not going to try to figure out the dynamics of this crazy relationship you have with Will McCaffrey. Just know that if things work out for you, I'll be the happiest person in the world. And if they don't, I'll be there to help pick up the pieces." She stood and grabbed the keys to the truck. "But for now, I've got to go pick up those twinkle lights before I head home. How are you getting to work tomorrow?"

"Since you're taking the truck, you're going to pick me up," Jane said. "Make it early, so I can—"

"Avoid sharing a bathroom with Will?"

"No, so we can stop by the office before we head out to the job."

"You're not going to be able to avoid him forever," Lisa said.

"I'm determined to avoid him whenever I can, especially at moments when my face is blotchy and my hair looks like it was styled with a hedge-trimmer. I do have some pride, you know."

Lisa's eyebrow rose. "I'd think you'd want to look as bad as you can. Aren't you supposed to be the fiancée from hell?"

"Go pick up those lights," Jane said, knowing if she kept talking to Lisa, she'd talk herself into the truth about her feelings—feelings that were a bit more intense than she was ready to admit.

She turned back to the liver, simmering on the stove. When she lifted the cover, the smell wafted through the room again and she gagged slightly. God, she hated liver, but it was well worth the "ick" factor just to see his face as he cut into the leathery meat.

Jane felt a nudge at her leg and she glanced down to find Thurgood sitting next to the stove. "You want a taste?" He wagged his tail and "woofed" softly. Jane picked a small piece out of the pan and set it on a saucer in front of the dog. Thurgood bent down to sniff at it, then looked back up at her as if she'd just insulted him. He sighed, then got up and walked away, plop-ping down in front of the door.

"Well, if the dog won't eat it, then I guess it's done."

WILL PUSHED HIS KEY INTO the lock and opened the back door, shrugging out of his coat as he stepped inside. The stereo played softly and Thurgood trotted up to greet him, nuzzling his nose against Will's hand. He bent down and rubbed the fur behind the dog's ears before he straightened. "Hey, buddy, what have you been up to all day?"

Will opened his mouth to call out and then saw Jane in the kitchen. Just the sight of her washed away all the troubles of his day. He had an entire evening to look forward to and suddenly he understood one of the major benefits of marriage—a comforting and happy place to come home to at the end of the day.

"Honey, I'm home," he called.

Jane jumped in surprise, then spun around. She pressed her hand to her heart. "You scared me!"

Will tossed his coat over the back of the family-room sofa as he strolled toward her. God, she was pretty. She wore a pair of khaki trousers and a white Oxford blouse that fit her perfectly, molding to her narrow waist and perfect breasts. He fought the urge to sweep her into his arms and kiss her, ridding her of the silly little apron she wore before he started on the rest of her clothes. "You made dinner." He sniffed. "What is that smell?"

"Liver and onions."

He bit back a gasp and forced a smile. "Liver and on-ions? We're having liver for dinner?"

Jane nodded enthusiastically. "Yes. Now that I'm here to take care of you, I'm going to make it my job to see that you eat properly. No more beer and potato chips. Ice cream is out—too high in fat and cholesterol. And those frozen pizzas are loaded with salt. Now that you're over thirty, you have to start watching your blood pressure." She grabbed two plates and a handful of silverware and walked into the dining room.

"You're making me feel old," Will said, leaning back against the edge of the counter.

"But you are old." Jane walked back into the kitchen. "You're going to be a married man and you know what happens when you get married."

Will noted the earnest expression on her face and wasn't sure he wanted to hear what happened when a guy got married. Especially if it had anything to do with organ meats. "What is that?"

"Middle-age spread. I personally think there's nothing wrong with little love handles, but I draw the line at a pot belly."

Will's hand dropped to his stomach and he rubbed it through his starched white shirt. "I work out."

"Of course you do. But now that we're together, you're not going to have the extra time to spend at the gym, honey."

"I'm not?"

"No," she said, shaking her head. "Couples need to spend all their extra time together. We have to work on our relationship, really get to know each other like no one else does. We need to talk."

"About what?"

"Our relationship. We need to grow as a couple. You

know what they say. Marriage means that two people become one. And if we're going to be one, then we have to start thinking as one, don't you agree?"

Hell, yesterday Jane had been ready to bolt and now she was talking about marriage as if it were inevitable—and she made it sound a little bit frightening as well. This had to be part of the little game she was playing, this back and forth dance they'd engaged in. A niggling fear twisted in his gut. Or maybe she *was* this enthusiastic about marriage. "I—I guess."

She picked up the pan from the stove, grabbed a towel and headed back to the dining room. "Dinner is served."

Reluctantly Will wandered to the dinner table. She'd pulled out the chair at the head of the table and had already ladled a large portion of liver onto his plate by the time he sat down.

"So, what do you think of dinner?" She handed him a covered casserole. "We have boiled beets and there's a salad with lemon juice dressing and for dessert, wheat-germ surprise."

Will glanced over at her plate, noticing that all she'd dished up for herself was lettuce and a few beets. "Aren't you going to have some liver?"

"No, I'm just going to have veggies. I have to watch my figure now, too. After the babies, it's always hard to shed those extra pounds."

Will choked on the piece of liver he was chewing, then snatched up his water and gulped it down. Babies? Jeez, she knew all the right buttons to push! But he wasn't going to let her see him sweat. "You have a beautiful body just the way it is," Will said. He glanced over to see a blush creep up her cheeks.

When he'd finally managed to swallow the liver, he understood why it was considered a healthy meal. After one bite, a guy didn't feel like eating anything else for the rest of the evening. He'd never tasted anything quite so vile. But he knew Jane had probably worked hard to make their first dinner special—or had she?

The bottle of wine that accompanied the meal went a long way toward washing down the main course and when he'd finally finished the last bite of liver, Will was feeling the effects of the wine. He sat back in his chair and rubbed his stomach. "That was...great," he lied. "Very nutritious. I feel better already, all that iron. I feel like Superman. I could leap tall buildings in a...well, you know what I mean."

"There's plenty left," she said.

Will shook his head. "No. Why don't you save the leftovers? I'll take them to work tomorrow for my lunch."

"If you like it so much, we can have liver night," Jane said.

His stomach roiled and he took a long swallow of his wine. "Liver night?"

She nodded. "Yes. Sometimes married couples eat certain things on certain nights. Friday is pizza night, Thursday is salad night, Sunday is sandwich night. We could make Monday liver night."

"Could we hold off on that decision?" Will asked. "I'd like to try a few more of your culinary delights before we focus on just one. By the way, I'm a pretty decent cook. I hear some married couples trade off cooking duties." At least he'd be assured of a decent meal fifty percent of the time, Will mused.

"Oh, no. I really think it's my duty to do the cooking," Jane insisted, a little too enthusiastically. Will didn't know much about marriage, but he sure as hell knew that any working wife would jump at the chance to share some of the household responsibilities. And either she was deliberately goading him or he'd let a crazy woman move into his house. Will was pretty sure Jane had ulterior motives for acting like an enthusiastic wife. He just hadn't figured out what they were yet.

He reached across the table and took her hand, lacing his fingers through hers. "I really would like to help."

She quickly stood, tugging her fingers from his, her mood shifting in the blink of an eye. "I—I should clean up."

"I'll help."

"No!" She paused, clutching at her apron. "I'll do it. You—you finish your dessert."

She quickly gathered the plates from the table. He had to say that he'd enjoyed looking across the dinner table at Jane. He usually ate at the kitchen counter, scarfing down whatever frozen dinner he'd managed to microwave that night. And it was nice to have her in the house, to listen to her moving around, clattering pots and pans in the kitchen.

"How are you doing in there?" Will called. "Are you sure you don't want a little help?"

"No, I'm fine."

"I should tell you that—"

Before he had a chance to warn her about the tricky garbage disposal, a scream echoed through the house. Will shoved back from the table and rushed into the kitchen. Janie stood at the sink, her face and blouse smeared with brown goo.

"It—it just exploded!" she wailed, the ground-up liver dripping from her hands and nose.

Will bit back a laugh and grabbed a kitchen towel. "I forgot to warn you," he said. He turned her to face him and gently wiped the goo from her cheeks. "That little rubber thing always flies out of the drain when you first turn it on. You have to hold it down."

"Oh, yuck," she said, shaking the drippy mess off her hands.

"Don't be such a baby," Will teased. "We just ate that yuck."

"I've ruined my blouse."

"I'll buy you another blouse." As he brushed the towel over her hair, Will couldn't contain himself and began to chuckle. "God, this stuff smells as bad as it tastes."

She looked up at him, her eyes wide. "I thought you liked it."

Will stared down at her, his gaze skimming over her pretty features. She'd changed so much over the years, but there were still moments when he saw the girl he once knew. He dragged the towel across her lips. And then, without thinking, he leaned forward and traced the same path with his mouth, lingering for a long moment. It should have been over then, a gentle show of affection, and nothing more. Instead the kiss was intoxicating, sending a rush of heat through his bloodstream to pool in his lap.

He'd thought about kissing her any number of times since he'd seen her on the street outside her office. But not once had he anticipated such a swift and sudden reaction. With a low groan, Will cupped her face in his hands and stared down into her eyes. A moment later, he found her mouth again. Rational thought seemed to leave his brain as he tasted her lips, damp and sweet and tinged with wine.

He waited for Jane to respond, to open beneath him, to give him the tiniest clue as to what she was feeling. And then, her arms slipped around his neck and she pressed up against his body, and Will knew that kissing her hadn't been a mistake.

Tracing her lips with his tongue, he teased her into surrender, taking his chance to explore the warmth beyond her lips. A tiny sigh slipped from her throat as his hand moved from her cheeks to tangle in her hair, forcing her to meet his tongue with her own.

Will had kissed his fair share of women, but he couldn't recall it ever feeling quite like this. He wanted to possess her completely, to strip away everything between them except the realities of need and desire. He spun her around and pressed her back against the refrigerator, molding her mouth to his, pressing his body along the length of hers until he couldn't tell where he left off and she began. And though his mind whirled with wild sensations and his body ached with unbidden passion, Will knew that for now, this was as far as he could take it. This kiss, this sweet heat between them, this silent communication that seemed to speak their secret thoughts, would be over in just a few more seconds.

When her hands drifted down to the buttons of his shirt and began to work at them, Will groaned softly. He gently grabbed her fingers, lacing them through his. Once she started in on his clothes, he wasn't sure he'd find a way to stop, so he wrapped his arms around her waist, trapping her hands behind her back.

He'd always rushed headlong into seduction, anxious for the inevitable release. Maybe that had been his problem all along, his focus on physical pleasures and nothing more. He wanted more with Jane and for the first time in his life, he believed he might find it.

For now, this kiss was enough, just a taste of what they might share in the future. When he finally drew away, he stared down at her, stuck by the incredible beauty of her face. Jane's eyes were closed, her lashes dark against her cheeks, her lips damp and slightly swollen.

"Why don't I finish straightening up the kitchen while you go clean up?" he murmured, stealing one last kiss.

She opened her eyes and blinked before her hands flitted to her hair. "Sorry about the mess," she said.

Will smoothed his palm over her cheek and grinned. "No problem. You look cute with liver in your hair."

She gave him a coy smile, then turned and walked out of the kitchen. Will let out a long breath and leaned back against the edge of the counter. All night long she'd been hiding behind this strange facade of the proper mate. And then in an instant, she'd gone from wifely into wanton. What the hell was she doing to him? When he was with Jane he felt as if he were venturing into unknown territory. Though she was a woman, she wasn't like any woman he'd ever been with before.

Shaking his head, Will set to mopping up the brown goo from the counter and the floor. Life promised to be a lot more interesting with Janie in the house. As he rinsed out a kitchen towel, he heard the shower go on upstairs and paused. An image flashed in his mind, Jane stripping off her clothes, Jane stepping beneath the rush of water, Jane—

Will cleared his throat and turned his attention back to more mundane matters. Sure, there was a naked woman just upstairs, but she might as well have been on the moon for all the good it did him. Seducing Jane at this point in their relationship would be a big mistake.

But some night it might happen. He'd kiss her and look into her eyes and know that neither one of them wanted to stop. He'd give her the pleasure she deserved and the release he craved. But until then, he'd have to tread carefully because Jane Singleton had an uncanny way of making him forget they were friends and not lovers.

4

"I'LL SEE YOU TOMORROW MORNING," Jane said as she jumped out of the pickup truck. "Come by early. I need to drop off some money at the auto mechanic before we go to the job site. He's still holding my car hostage. And the longer it stays there, the more he finds wrong with it."

"Why don't you just keep the truck?" Lisa asked.

"Because, if I make you come all the way over here to pick me up and we have to drive all the way over to Wicker Park to pick up our equipment, I have to leave the house at 6:00 a.m., thereby avoiding breakfast with Will."

"You're avoiding him already. I take it your plan isn't going too well?"

"He loves everything I make," Jane cried, her frustration filling her voice. "The night before last I made fishstick casserole. God, it was awful. And last night I made tofu burgers. It was like eating cottage cheese on a bun. But he just smiled and complimented me on the menu. Either he has an iron stomach or he's playing me."

"Or maybe he's just being a sweet guy and doesn't want to hurt your feelings? What's on the menu for tonight?"

Jane grinned. "We're having gourmet tonight. Badly overcooked risotto, guaranteed to taste like wallpaper paste. I think it's time to move into phase two of the plan. Major redecorating. I'm thinking of going with a whole magenta theme mixed with lots of lace and ruffles. Think Victorian dollhouse meets French bordello. When I get done with his house, he'll be finished with me for good."

"And that's what you want, right?" Lisa asked.

Jane nodded. "Right," she murmured, her mind flashing back to the kiss they'd shared a few nights before. She slammed the truck door and walked toward the front steps of Will's house, glancing over her shoulder at Lisa to wave goodbye. As she watched the truck disappear down the street, Jane sat down on the steps and stared out at the tree-lined street.

After four nights in Will's house, Jane was reaching the point of exhaustion. She'd had to work so hard to keep her guard up, to maintain a distance from him and to resist his charms. Jane had worried she'd be faced with the same problem every night—his lips waiting there for her lips to bump into them.

She sighed softly. Even though she might have welcomed another kiss, Will hadn't seemed anxious to repeat the experience—and he'd had plenty of opportunities. Obviously he hadn't enjoyed the experience as much as she had. Or maybe, after all the women he'd had, kissing just didn't rock his boat the way it did hers. Jane closed her eyes and tried to replay the moment in her mind.

It had been incredible, a twenty-seven on a scale of

one to ten. The kiss had been sweet and gentle, warm and tantalizing, and arousing and astonishing all at once—and mixed with enough passion to make her want to keep kissing him for the rest of the night. She'd been surprised at first because it hadn't been anything like the kiss they'd shared six years ago. That long-ago kiss had become an event of mythic proportions in her mind. The more recent kiss was so real that it made her heart race just thinking about it.

A shiver raced through her body and she rubbed her arms through her jacket. How much longer could she do this? Every night, staring at him from across the dinner table, watching him while he took in a football game, imagining him asleep in his bed while she lay awake in hers. It hadn't even been a week and she felt as if she was ready to crack under the pressure of wanting him.

"Maybe it's time to call a lawyer," Jane murmured. If she could find a way out of the contract, then she wouldn't have to worry about the next eleven weeks. She could walk out whenever their little "engagement" became too much to bear, which might be sooner than later if he decided to kiss her again...

"Or maybe not," she murmured.

There was another option. According to their agreement, they had three months together. She could always throw caution to the wind and jump into a passionate affair with him. She could see what a man like Will McCaffrey was like...sexually. She could give herself the kind of experience she might not ever have with another man. And then she could walk away, no strings, no regrets and lots of really good memories.

"Janie? What are you doing sitting out here?"

Jane twisted around and watched Will walk out the front door. He jogged down the steps and sat down beside her, his shoulder brushing up against hers. "How long have you been out here?" he asked.

"Not long. Lisa just dropped me off."

"Hard day at work?" he asked.

Jane shrugged. "A lot of fall cleanup." She stretched her arms out in front of her, working the kinks out of a stiff back. "It always makes me a little sad when I realize that winter is coming. All the other times of the year have something to look forward to. In spring, it's all the planning and the planting. In the summer, watching everything grow. And in the fall, everything reaches its peak. And then it freezes and it's all over for six months."

"I've been waiting for you," Will said. He shifted up to the step behind her and drew her back between his legs, his hands gently kneading her shoulders. Jane closed her eyes and bit back a low moan, the feel of his hands on her body sending her senses into overdrive. Did he realize how disarming his impromptu massage was?

"Janie?"

"Mmm?"

"I think I may have made a tiny mistake."

"No, that feels good," she murmured. "A little to the left. There—right there."

"Your mother called."

She stiffened, then twisted around to look at Will. "My mother?" Jane scrambled to her feet. "How did she—why is she—she doesn't know I'm—" She stumbled down the steps and paced back and forth on the sidewalk.

"It's my fault," Will admitted, jumping down in front of her. He smoothed his hands over her arms and she found his touch strangely calming. "I guess you had your home phone transferred over to my number and when I picked up, she asked who I was. So I told her."

An uneasy feeling gripped her stomach. "What did you tell her?"

"I told her I was Will McCaffrey—your fiancé?" he replied, wincing. "I wasn't sure what you'd told your parents."

Jane groaned as she sat back down on the front steps, pressing the heels of her hands to her temples. This was all she needed! She was having enough trouble maneuvering around this crazy situation without getting consumed by the possibilities of romance. Adding her mother to the mix was like throwing gasoline on an already raging fire. Selma Singleton was merciless when it came to her daughter's romantic prospects. She'd been so desperate for Jane to have a date to her junior prom that she'd actually paid a boy to take her.

"And she's inside," Will added.

"You told her where you lived?" Jane screeched.

"Sweetie, she's your mother. Don't you think she has a right to know?"

Jane wagged a finger at him accusingly. "Don't call

me sweetie! And don't you dare side with my mother. You don't know my mother. She's been waiting for me to get married ever since I turned eighteen. It's her dream to plan a big, splashy wedding. She has scrapbooks filled with gowns and cakes and flowers. She's subscribed to three different bridal magazines since I was in high school and every year, she makes a reservation for the ballroom at their country club for the second week in June. She's obsessed!"

"You're talking like I've unleashed the forces of hell," he said.

Jane stood and trudged up the steps to the front door. "Selma Singleton makes Beelzebub look like Mother Teresa."

She reached for the doorknob, but the door swung open in front of her. "Darling!" Her mother bustled out, dressed in her favorite pink Chanel suit and her pearls, and dragged Jane into her embrace. "Oh, Janie, why didn't you call and tell me your fabulous news? Imagine my surprise when I had to meet your fiancé over the phone."

"He's not really my fiancé, Mom."

"I'm not?" Will asked.

"Don't be silly," Selma said, fussing with Jane's hair the same way she had when Jane was a child. "Of course he is." She reached out and slipped an arm around Will's waist, pulling them both into a group hug. "Let's go inside and talk about the wedding." She looked at them both and suddenly, her face crumpled. "I'm sorry," she said, waving her hand. "This is such a precious moment. I've waited so long for this. My sweet girl has found the man of her dreams. It's like a fairy tale come true." Selma grabbed both their hands and steered them into the house.

Jane glanced over at her "fiancé" and he sent her an apologetic, but slightly terrified smile.

"We have a few minutes to talk before Margaret Delancy arrives," Selma said, drawing them into the living room and perching on the edge of the sofa. "I want you to tell me all the details. What do you do for a living, Will? Where is your family from? How did you two meet? And why doesn't my daughter have an engagement ring?"

At this, Will chuckled softly. "I guess we just haven't gotten around to buying one yet."

Jane sat down in a leather wing chair near Will's leather sofa and Will stood behind her, his hand resting on her shoulder. "Mom, who is Margaret Delancy?"

"This is a lovely house," Selma gushed. "So much room. I imagined that you'd be living in a tiny flat. Just like *Barefoot in the Park*." She turned to her daughter. "Robert Redford, Jane Fonda. Such a romantic movie. But there's plenty of room here for grandchildren." She paused, then pressed her fingers to her lips as if she was about to cry again.

Jane jumped to her feet and sat down next to her mother, patting her hand. "Who is Margaret Delancy?" she repeated, distracting Selma's attention.

"She's a wedding planner, dear. As soon as I heard the good news, I called her and she agreed to come over and talk with us. She'll be here in a few minutes."

"You invited her here?"

"It pays to be organized, dear. She'll help us work out all the little details. I want your special day to be perfect, don't you?" She reached out and took Jane's face between her hands. "You're going to be such a beautiful bride. Isn't she going to be beautiful, Will? Oh, I think I'm getting misty again. Will, fetch me a tissue, would you? I never have a hankie when I need one."

Jane glanced back and forth between her mother and Will. Compared to her mother's expression of utter rapture and Will's bemused smile, Jane could only muster a chronic case of dread. This was not going as planned. Her mother's arrival had thrown a major wrench into the works. Jane cocked her head in the direction of the kitchen. "Mom, if you'll excuse us, I have to talk to my fiancé for a moment."

Grabbing Will's arm, she dragged him out of the living room. "What?" he murmured.

"Why don't you say something to her?"

"Say what? If you haven't noticed, it's a little hard to get a word in edgewise. Every time she looks at me, she starts to cry. And what am I supposed to tell her? It sounds like she has a real good handle on the wedding plans."

"Tell her to go away and take her wedding planner with her."

He shrugged. "Maybe you should listen to what she has to say. From what I understand, planning a wedding can be very time-consuming, Jane. And you're working full-time."

Jane gasped, then slapped his shoulder. "I'm not going to start planning our wedding! We haven't even made it through one week together much less three months. And I haven't agreed to marry you. This is just a trial engagement. In fact, it's not really an engagement at all."

He met her gaze. "So you're not even considering it might work out between us?"

She opened her mouth to reply, then snapped it shut. "Are—are you?"

"I'm certainly giving it a chance," he said.

Jane swallowed hard. "You are?"

"Of course. And I thought you were, too. What harm could it do? Just talk to her. And try to keep her from crying."

The doorbell rang and Jane jumped at the sound. Will reached out and took her hand, drawing it toward him and holding it to his chest. Jane could feel his heartbeat beneath her fingers and she closed her eyes and gathered her resolve. Day by day, he seemed to chip away at her defenses, leaving her to wonder if maybe they could find something special together.

Will hooked a finger beneath her chin and tilted her gaze to meet his. Slowly he leaned forward and touched his lips to hers in a kiss so warm and sweet that Jane felt as if she were melting into him. She sighed softly and he wrapped his arms around her waist, accepting her unspoken invitation to take more.

His tongue traced the crease of her mouth and she surrendered to the gentle assault and opened beneath it. This was what she remembered about their last kiss, this whirlwind of sensation that seemed to lift her off her feet and make her dizzy with desire. A low moan rumbled in Will's chest and the kiss grew more intense, their tastes mingling, their tongues tangling, his hands furrowing through her hair.

"Oh, would you look at that!"

Jane quickly stepped out of Will's embrace, her fingers trembling as she touched her damp lips. Selma stood in the entrance to the kitchen with her wedding planner, smiles beaming.

"Sorry," Jane murmured.

"Aren't they the most handsome couple?" Selma said. "My grandchildren are going to be beautiful. Come on, now. Let's go sit down and we'll discuss the wedding."

Her mother had always approached every one of her projects with unbridled enthusiasm. Whether it was her charity work or her rose garden or her determination to learn golf, Selma Singleton wouldn't quit until she'd achieved perfection. And now in a way, Jane felt as if she could make a dream come true for her mother. She'd fuss over the proper flowers and the perfect dress, the best style of invitation and the most popular table favors, caught up in the magic of a perfect wedding.

But how would her mother feel when she learned there wasn't going to be a wedding? Jane opened her mouth, ready to tell her the truth, determined to nip the wedding plans in the bud. But Will's voice cut in.

"Mrs. Singleton—"

"Selma," she insisted. "Or Mother, if you prefer."

She pressed her lips together, fighting another wave of emotion. "Mother. You can call me Mother."

"Selma will be fine," Will said. "If you don't mind, I think we'll have to do this another time. Jane just got home from work and I know she's had a very long day. Why don't we call you tomorrow and schedule a meeting?" He stepped over to her mother and put his arm around her shoulders, steering her toward the front door. "I can see how much energy this is going to take and Jane will want to be at her best, don't you think?"

"Of course," Selma said in an apologetic tone. "But maybe we could begin with just a few simple details? Sweetheart, what is your favorite flower?"

"Jane's favorite flower is the English rose. She prefers them in yellow or creamy white."

"And what about the bridesmaid dresses?" the bridal planner asked. "We have to decide on a direction there. And the cake, what about the cake?"

"Jane would probably like simple but elegant dresses, nothing frilly. And her favorite flavor of cake would be chocolate, but she's also partial to banana." He turned back to her. "Right?"

She nodded, astonished that he knew. Had he simply been guessing and gotten lucky? Or had he tucked away this mundane knowledge of her long ago. "Right," she murmured. "I'd like a banana cake."

Jane's breath froze in her throat and had she been able to reach out and snatch the words back, she would have. Oh, good grief! She'd like a banana wedding cake? She wasn't supposed to want *any* wedding cake—no wedding, no groom, no happily-ever-after—

at least not with Will McCaffrey. Yet in a heartbeat, she'd been swept away by the fantasy.

"Then we've decided," Will said. "Banana. With that frosting, that—"

They both said "cream cheese" at exactly the same time and Jane bit her bottom lip.

"And what about the colors?" the wedding planner asked.

Jane looked at Will, waiting for him to answer, daring him to know her favorite color. "I think Jane looks beautiful in the palest shades of lavender," he said. "She has a sweater she wears that I like and it's a color that sets off her eyes and skin and goes perfectly with her dark hair."

Jane remembered the lavender sweater she was wearing the day they'd met on the street. It was her favorite sweater...in her favorite color. A tiny smile curled the corners of her mouth and a flood of affection warmed her heart. She didn't care if Will was too charming for his own good, he knew her favorite color and he all but said she was pretty.

For now, that was enough to make her seriously reconsider her "housewife from hell" plan.

"TELL ME AGAIN WHY WE'RE HERE?" Will asked.

Jane held tight to his hand as she pulled him toward the second-floor escalator at Bloomingdale's. She hated shopping and this trip was guaranteed to be sheer torture, but it had to be done. "Bridal registration." Sooner or later, Will had to crack and bridal registration had been known to drive a wedge between even the most loving couples.

Since her mother's visit, the wedding plans had begun in earnest. Her mother had called every day, anxious for more input. To Jane's relief, Selma had decided that they'd need at least a year to plan the big event, buying Jane enough time to break the bad news gently and before any large sums of money had been invested.

"I thought you didn't want to marry me," Will said, stopping short.

Jane turned and hitched her hands on her hips. "This is only to pacify my mother. She'll look at our list and then give her advice as to what we're missing. She'll have her opinions about French china and leaded crystal and shrimp forks and sugar tongs."

Will shrugged as they rode up the escalator. "So we're going to tell them we're getting married and they're going to tell us what we need?"

"No, we're going to tell them what we *want* for wedding presents," Jane explained. "We're going to pick out everything and then when someone wants to buy us a gift, they just come here and look at the list we made."

"Cool," Will said. "I like that. So we're not going to get ten toasters and a lava lamp?"

"We're not going to get anything," Jane reminded him. "This is just an exercise because I haven't decided to marry you."

"Yet," he said as he threw his arm around her shoulders and pulled her against him. "Yeah, you're likin' me pretty much, aren't you? Come on, you can admit it. I'm a nice guy and you can't resist me, can you?"

He didn't know the truth of his words, Jane mused. Yes, she was liking him a lot. As each day passed, she had more and more trouble convincing herself Will wasn't the most perfect man in the world. But then she'd remind herself that every one of his girlfriends had thought the very same thing—until he'd dumped them, leaving them confused and brokenhearted. "You are a nice guy," Jane admitted. "I'm not immune to your charm."

"And I haven't pulled out my best weapons yet."

Jane pondered what he meant as they rode to the top floor on the escalators, then slowly strolled through the china and crystal departments. There were so many choices it gave Jane a headache just to think about it. No wonder brides went postal on a regular basis. The sales associate from bridal registry explained the choices they'd have to make, then handed Jane a clipboard.

"Let's start with something easy," Jane said. "Sheets and towels."

Will followed her to the domestics department. Jane glanced at him over her shoulder and found him frowning at the stacks and stacks of Egyptian-cotton bath towels in a rainbow of color choices. She grabbed a bright pink towel and held it out to him. "This one," she said.

He gave her a dubious look. "For you maybe, but I'm not going to wrap myself in that thing after I get out of the shower." He grabbed a towel in navy blue.

"I want this one. At least I can face myself in the mirror wearing this color."

Jane brushed aside an unbidden image of a naked Will wrapped in any towel—and then wrapped in no towel at all. She swallowed hard and wondered if Bloomie's had any see-through towels. "We have to choose just one. That's what marriage is all about. We're thinking as one. We have to learn to compromise."

"Right. And I have to compromise on hot pink towels?" Will said.

"They're watermelon, not hot pink. And if you were secure in your masculinity, you wouldn't have to worry about the kind of towel you were wearing."

Will opened his mouth, then snapped it shut. He grabbed her hand and pulled her along with him, behind a tall display of shower curtains. When they were hidden from the rest of the shoppers, Will cupped her face in his hands and kissed her, long and hard, his tongue teasing at her lips until she returned the kiss with equal passion.

Jane thought he would stop there, but then he brushed her jacket aside and slipped his hands around her hips and beneath her sweater. When his cool palms met her warm skin, she sucked in a sharp breath and pressed herself closer, inviting him to take more. She knew there were shoppers nearby, knew they risked being seen, but Jane couldn't seem to stop herself. The danger of discovery only added to the excitement.

His hands slipped up until he cupped her breasts, teasing at her nipples through the lacy fabric of her bra.

A delicious ache settled into her belly and she moaned softly, urging him on while she tugged his shirt from the waistband of his jeans. Her hands found his belly, flat and muscular, with a soft dusting of hair, and then dropped lower. She brushed up against his erection, hot and hard beneath the denim.

Will nuzzled her neck then kissed his way up to her ear. "I don't think we need to question my masculinity," he whispered.

Jane's eyes snapped open and she looked up at him to find him grinning at her. With a growl of frustration, she stepped away from him and quickly restored order to her clothes. "You are not *that* charming," she said, stalking back out to the center of the sales floor. "And we're getting the pink towels."

"Watermelon," he corrected.

She threw the towel at his head and grabbed the clipboard from where she'd dropped it. "I'm moving on to sheets."

"Good idea," he said. "Let's move onto the bed."

"Just because you can turn bridal registry into some sex game doesn't mean you're charming," she muttered.

He caught up with her and grabbed her hand, forcing her to a stop. "You think I don't know what you're doing? Come on, Janie, I'm not a fool. You think if you drive me crazy with your horrible cooking and tacky decorating, that I'm going to send you packing."

"My horrible cooking?" Jane shifted uneasily, embarrassed that he'd seen through her motives so quickly. She scrambled for an excuse, an alternative motivation, but she couldn't come up with anything that made sense.

"You forget," Will said, his voice low, "we used to have dinner all the time when we were in school. And you were an excellent cook. And I don't remember pink being your favorite color—ever."

He slowly stroked her cheek as he stared down into her eyes. For a moment, she thought he might kiss her again, but then he grinned mischievously. "Let's forget the sheets," Will said. "I have a much better idea." He pulled her along toward the elevator. "We need to pick out something much more important."

"What could be more important than sheets?" Jane asked.

"You'll see."

They waited for a few minutes before the doors opened, then Will pressed the button for the first floor and they rode down. When they stepped out, he took her hand again and began to search the sales floor. A moment later, they stood in front of a glass case, filled with diamond rings. "All right," he said. "You wanted a big diamond. Pick one."

Jane gasped. "What?"

"You heard me. Pick one. Any ring you want, it's yours."

"I'm not choosing an engagement ring."

"Why not?" Will asked, his eyebrow arching. "We're choosing sheets and towels for no good reason. But the ring was actually part of the deal, remember?" He nodded at the salesman who stood behind the counter, then pointed at a velvet-covered display of rings. "We'd like to see those."

"No, we wouldn't," Jane said, trying to pull away from Will. Picking out towels was one thing, but this was hitting a little to close to reality. Insisting on a big ring had just been the first salvo in a swiftly unraveling plan. She'd never really intended to force him into a purchase. "Let's go."

"No, I want you to pick one," he insisted. "Come on, it can't be that difficult. Every woman likes diamonds."

She met his gaze, stubbornly refusing to give in. "I'm not every woman."

His expression softened and Will smiled. "No, you're not. I'm beginning to realize that."

"But if I was," she said, "I'd choose this one." She pointed to a huge emerald-cut diamond set in platinum. "Now if you're finished kidding around, I'm going to go back upstairs to pick out some bed linens."

Jane turned and started toward the escalators again, but Will remained behind to speak to the salesperson. A few moments later, he came up behind her, slipping his hands around her waist. "We're not choosing pink bed sheets," he said. "I'm putting my foot down."

Jane smiled to herself. "That doesn't sound like compromise to me."

"I don't have to do any compromising until we're married," he muttered. "Until then, there will be no more pink in my house, no more of that smelly potpourri stuff in the bathroom and no more tofu burgers."

The Harlequin Reader Service® — Here's how it works:

Accepting your 2 free books and gift places you under no obligation to buy anything. You may keep the books and gift and return the shipping statement marked "cancel." If you do not cancel, about a month later we'll send you 4 additional books and bill you just $3.57 each in the U.S., or $4.24 each in Canada, plus 25¢ shipping & handling per book and applicable taxes if any.* That's the complete price and — compared to cover prices of $4.25 each in the U.S. and $4.99 each in Canada — it's quite a bargain! You may cancel at any time, but if you choose to continue, every month we'll send you 4 more books, which you may either purchase at the discount price or return to us and cancel your subscription.

*Terms and prices subject to change without notice. Sales tax applicable in N.Y. Canadian residents will be charged applicable provincial taxes and GST.

If offer card is missing write to: The Harlequin Reader Service, 3010 Walden Ave., P.O. Box 1867, Buffalo, NY 14240-1867

BUSINESS REPLY MAIL
FIRST-CLASS MAIL   PERMIT NO. 717-003   BUFFALO, NY

POSTAGE WILL BE PAID BY ADDRESSEE

NO POSTAGE
NECESSARY
IF MAILED
IN THE
UNITED STATES

HARLEQUIN READER SERVICE
3010 WALDEN AVE
PO BOX 1867
BUFFALO NY 14240-9952

WILL OPENED THE TINY VELVET BOX and stared at the diamond ring. He'd been carrying it around for two days, trying to decide when to give it to Jane. It probably hadn't been the best purchase, considering Jane's true motives had finally been revealed. This little game they'd been playing had come to an end and there was nothing left now but the reality of their situation.

Every time they kissed, Will found himself drowning in a flood of confusion. What had begun as a simple friendship had suddenly turned complicated, desire mixing with emotion until he wasn't sure what he really wanted.

And then there was Jane. Just what did she want? Every time he kissed her, he didn't feel as though he was kissing a woman bent on destroying their tenuous relationship. He kissed a woman who wanted him as much as he wanted her.

He leaned back in his office chair, holding the diamond up to the light. The intimacies between them were growing, the kisses they'd shared becoming increasingly more intense. Last night, a simple kiss had resulted in an entire evening of necking on the sofa.

Though Will had decided not to push her, he wasn't sure how much more he could take. They were both normal adults with normal needs. He let his thoughts wander, imagining the circumstances that might lead to seduction. Though he'd thought about walking into her bedroom and offering up his "services," Jane would probably expect something on a grand romantic scale, just like one of her Audrey Hepburn movies.

First, he'd have to kiss her thoroughly, wearing

down her doubts and insecurities, leaving her breathless and wanting more. Then he'd have to tell her how he felt, in words that were memorable and somewhat literate. And only then would he be able to sweep her into his arms and carry her to his bed. Once they got into the bedroom, Will was fairly certain he'd know what to do.

A sharp rap interrupted his thoughts and he looked up to find his father standing in the office doorway. "I had a phone call last night," he said.

Will quickly snapped the box shut and tucked it into his jacket pocket. "Are you waiting for me to guess who it was from?"

"You don't know?"

"No," Will said warily. "But I suspect you're about to tell me."

"Your future mother-in-law called. She wanted to invite the family for Thanksgiving. At first, I thought she was just some crazy woman, but when she told me my son, Will McCaffrey, was engaged to her daughter, Jane Singleton, I was forced to consider she might be telling me the truth. Are you engaged?"

Will wasn't sure how to answer that question. Legally he could claim he and Jane had made an agreement to marry. But until she actually professed her undying love for him, Will preferred to think they were "temporarily attached," and not quite fully engaged. But for professional purposes, Will didn't have to answer honestly. "That's what you wanted, isn't it?"

"I wanted you to get serious about your life," Jim

McCaffrey said. "Are you serious about this engagement?"

"Yeah, I am," Will said. The moment he said the words, he realized he was serious—maybe not about the engagement, but about Jane. It wasn't a lie to placate his father. He was beginning to believe he'd met the perfect woman years ago—and it had taken him all this time to find her again.

"And you're not going to dump this one like you've dumped all those others."

"I can't promise you there won't be difficult times," Will said. "But you were right. It's time that I started to take my life more seriously."

His father nodded. "So who is this girl?"

"Her name is Jane Singleton," Will explained. "We knew each other in college. She was a sophomore when I was in my last year of law school. She lived in the apartment above me."

"What kind of girl is she?"

"What the hell is that supposed to mean?" Will asked, his temper flaring. "And what difference does it make anyway? You want me married and I'm going to get married. Who I marry shouldn't make a difference."

His father cursed softly. "I want you to marry a woman you love, Will. I want you to be happy."

"And what you want for me has always been more important than what I want for me."

"We're not going to get into this again," he warned. "Do you want me to accept this invitation or not?"

"I don't know." Will pushed up from his desk and

walked to the sofa, grabbing his coat from where he'd tossed it earlier that afternoon. "I don't know what we have planned for the holidays. I'll talk to my fiancée and let you know."

He walked past his father, quelling the urge to goad him into an argument, to dump all his frustration on the person responsible for this whole crazy plan. As Will walked to his car, he tried to figure out why he was so angry. Was it because of the demands his father had made on him, the blatant manipulation and the ridiculous expectations? Or was it that he didn't want to be reminded of what had originally brought Jane back into his life?

Everything had seemed so simple a few weeks ago. He'd use the contract to get Jane back into his life and prove to his father he could find a girl worth marrying—even if he didn't marry her. But his growing feelings for Jane were anything but simple. They were confusing and amazing and powerful, and completely unexpected.

As he drove home, Will tried to put some order to his thoughts. With every block that passed, the anticipation of seeing her again increased. When did feelings like these fade or disappear? Every afternoon, he looked forward to walking into his house, enjoyed having someone there at the end of the day besides Thurgood. Even when it meant eating one of Jane's amazingly bad dinner creations or listening to her discuss the details of her redecorating plans, it was still worth it. And now that Jane's cooking had improved considerably and her manic obsession with pink had been stopped dead in its tracks, he'd started to leave work an hour early each day, just to be there when she got home.

When he pulled into the garage, he found Jane's Windy City pickup parked inside. He switched off the ignition and slipped out of the car, whistling softly as he walked through the connecting hallway into the house. When he got inside, Thurgood greeted him with a soft woof. Will bent down and scratched the dog's ears, then noticed something on his nose. "What is this? Have you been digging in the dirt again?"

He slowly stood and walked through the kitchen to the living room, Thurgood trotting after him. "Jane?" The lower floor of the house was silent. He took the stairs two at a time and wandered down the hall to her bedroom door. "Jane?"

"Go away," she said.

Her voice sounded shaky and strained. Will knocked softly on the door, then slowly pushed it open. He stopped short at the scene in front of him. "What the hell happened here?"

5

JANE IMPATIENTLY WIPED the tears from her cheeks and stood up. "It's nothing. I—I forgot to close my bedroom door this morning and Thurgood got in here. I guess he likes houseplants as much as I do."

She'd come home to a scene out of a horror movie—at least to her it looked like Nightmare on Winston Street. Her plants lay on the floor, yanked violently out of their pots, their roots exposed, dirt strewn everywhere. At first, she'd tried to save them, scooping up the dirt with her hands. But then emotions had overcome her and she'd sat down on the floor and cried.

"He chewed on all of them, except for the philodendron. Of course, that's the only poisonous one." Jane bent down and picked up Regina, the burro tail. Fresh tears pressed at the corners of her eyes. "I've had this plant since I was eleven."

Will took the plant from her hand. "Isn't there something we can do?"

"Sure. I can repot them or take cuttings and root them."

"Then why are you crying?" he asked.

Jane covered her face with her hands and sobbed. "I—I don't know." In truth, she did know. She knew that with every day that passed, it became harder and harder to ignore her growing feelings for Will. He'd eaten her awful cooking and tolerated her questionable decorating taste. He'd teased her out of her grumpy moods and had done his best to encourage her in everything she did. He knew her better than any man on the planet, and yet she still couldn't allow herself to love him.

She bit back a sob, then let her hands drop to her sides. Will knelt in front of her, staring into her face, his brow etched with concern. "I'm sorry. I didn't know Thurgood would do something like this. I've never had any plants around. He loves to dig outside. I guess I should have known."

Jane fixed her gaze on his mouth and all she could think about was how much she wanted him to kiss her again. Everything always seemed so much better when she was caught in his arms, his mouth taking possession of hers. She swallowed hard and clutched her hands in front of her. "I—I should have closed the door."

"Tell me what I should do," Will said. He gently rubbed his hands up and down her calves, a comforting caress that she found far too tantalizing. For a moment, Jane closed her eyes and tried to summon her resolve, tried to put up the barriers that had kept her safe from her desires.

"You don't have to do anything," Jane replied in a weak voice.

"I want to. Just tell me what you want me to do."

She groaned inwardly, knowing that her answer would have nothing at all to do with plants. Why was she fighting so hard? For once in her life, she had the chance to experience real passion, to be with a man who represented her ultimate sexual fantasy. And she still couldn't bring herself to make the first move, to put her needs and desires above the strict code of feminine conduct that her mother had instilled in her. She wanted him to kiss her again. And she didn't want him to stop for a very long time. And if they ended up tearing each other's clothes off and making love, she wouldn't object to that, either.

"Jane?"

She blinked and caught herself staring at his mouth. "What?"

Will straightened, then grabbed her hand and gently led her out of the room. "Come on," he said, dragging her across the hall to his bedroom. "Let's get you away from the carnage." He drew her down to sit on the edge of his bed, then sank down beside her. "Now, tell me what I can do to save the plants."

Oh, God. She was in his bedroom. If it happened, this was where it would happen. "You—you could put them in water," she murmured. "Or wrap them in wet paper towels. I'll have to get some potting soil and re-pot them."

"Why don't you just lie down here and relax and I'll take care of it? I could dig up some dirt from the neighbor's flower bed."

"That's the wrong kind of dirt," Jane said.

"There's more than one kind of dirt?" Will asked. "I thought dirt was dirt."

Jane nodded. "Garden dirt has all sorts of microbes and fungi and diseases in it. And it's not as friable as potting medium. It doesn't drain as well and—"

Will reached out and put his finger over her lips. "No garden dirt. I'll be right back."

Suddenly she felt exhausted, as if the whirl of desire and indecision was sapping every last ounce of her energy. Jane curled up on the bed and closed her eyes. Her mother's words ran through her head. "Why buy the cow when you can get the milk for free?" she murmured to herself. That's what her decision came down to. If she surrendered to her desire, would it signal the eventual end of Will's affections? Would she end up like all his other girlfriends—a part of his past?

She turned over and pressed her face into his pillow, the scent of his shampoo tickling at her nose. Wasn't that what she wanted? To put this relationship behind her once and for all? But if she made love to Will, she might never forget him, doomed to a life of existing on her memories. "I can't win," Jane said. "No matter what I do, I can't win."

God, why had she ever signed that contract? Why? Because she'd hoped someday he'd come to her, like a knight in shining armor, waving the contract in his hand and declaring his everlasting love. And though the fantasy seemed silly now, there was still a tiny bit of her heart that wanted it to be true, that wanted the fairy-tale ending.

She pinched her eyes shut, pushing such ridiculous thoughts from her head. She'd made a plan, a very sensible plan designed to protect her heart from Will McCaffrey's charm. All she had to do was stick to her strategy and she'd be safe. But she hadn't even spent two weeks with him and she was already an emotional wreck. "If things continue like this, I'm going to have to be institutionalized at the end of three months," Jane muttered.

She listened to Will moving around across the hall and decided to get up and help. But his bed was so comfortable and she just wasn't ready to face him yet, forced to cloak herself in indifference and pretend she didn't care. Instead she kept perfectly still, eyes closed, trying to steel her resolve and reconstruct the crumbling barriers she used to protect herself.

"I've cleaned up the mess."

His voice was soft and so close that she could feel the tickle of his breath on her cheek. Jane slowly opened her eyes to find him kneeling beside the bed.

"Although there are some critical injuries, I think all the patients are going to live. I got them back in their pots and gave them some water. They're sitting in the bathtub—with the bathroom door closed. I also had a stern talk with Thurgood and he promised he wouldn't be dining on your plants again."

Jane smiled weakly. "Thank you."

He reached out and ran a finger along her bottom lip. "There. That's better. I don't like seeing you cry. I know you love your plants and if any of them—"

"I wasn't crying about the plants," Jane murmured. "They're just plants."

Will frowned, his hand moving to stroke her cheek. "What then? Did I do something wrong?"

Jane took a ragged breath, torn between wanting to speak the truth and wanting to keep her feelings to herself. In the end, she chose the truth. "I've been trying really hard not to like you so much."

Her admission brought a smile and he leaned close,

his gaze capturing hers. "I sensed that. And how's that going for you?"

"Not so good," Jane admitted, tears filling her eyes again. "I didn't expect you to be so sweet to me."

"It's not difficult to be sweet to you, Janie." Will touched his lips to hers. A thrill raced through her body and Jane closed her eyes, allowing herself to enjoy the moment without hesitation. But it was over all too soon.

He pressed his forehead to hers and she tried to slow her racing pulse. How was it that a simple kiss from Will could elicit more passion than a full-scale seduction from any other man? He controlled her heart and now he'd taken control of her body, too. His lips were so close, tempting her to take just a little more, to lose herself in one more kiss.

"Are you all right now?"

Jane shook her head, drawing up her courage before she opened her eyes.

"What is it?" he asked.

For a moment, her voice refused to work. She swallowed hard. "Kiss me again."

He seemed surprised by her request, but didn't take any time considering his response. Leaning over the bed, he covered her mouth with his, this time softly taking her lower lip between his and gently sucking. Jane stifled a moan and wrapped her arms around his neck, pulling him off his knees and onto the bed.

The moment he sank down beside her, Jane knew. This was what she wanted and what she needed. She couldn't think about regrets, she couldn't think about anything that might happen in the future. The present was lying beside her and she was going to enjoy it while it lasted.

Will began a lazy exploration of her face, kissing her eyes and her nose and her chin, while his fingers twisted in her hair. Jane reveled in the flood of sensation that washed over her body and each time he came back to her mouth, she kissed him more deeply, a silent invitation to take more.

When he did, Jane arched up to meet his hands as they moved down her body, skimming along her rib cage to her waist. She reached down and yanked her blouse out of her jeans and Will immediately slipped his hands beneath, dragging her on top of him.

His touch was electric on her skin, the current pulsing through her flesh to warm her blood. Jane smoothed her hands over his chest and drifted up to his tie. She tugged at the silk, fumbling with the knot, and when she couldn't get it undone, Will rolled her over and got to his knees beside her.

His blue eyes searched her face and at first, Jane thought it was over, that he'd realized they'd gone too far. But then he tore at the tie and tossed it aside. She reached for the buttons on his shirt and taking her cue, he quickly pulled the shirt from his trousers and unbuttoned it himself. A moment later, he was back, stretched over her, the warmth of his body seeping through the thin cotton of her blouse.

She'd seen him nearly naked that first night, when she'd peeked into his bedroom. But looking at him from a distance was nothing compared to touching him. Smooth skin, hard muscle, it was all hers to explore and appreciate. Jane trailed kisses from his collarbone down his chest and when she teased at his nipple with her tongue, he shuddered. Raking his hands through her hair, Will gently drew her back to his mouth and this time, he kissed her like a man completely bent on seduction.

His tongue slipped in and out of her mouth, a tantalizing prelude to what they might share together. Jane didn't want to leave any doubt as to her desires. She found the buckle of his belt and undid it, knowing there was only one way to read her actions. She wanted him to make love to her. Her fingers worked the button open and reached for the zipper. But Will grabbed her wrist and drew back.

Jane glanced up into his gaze, startled by his expression. His jaw was tense and his eyes glazed with desire. "What do you want?" he whispered, pressing his mouth to the curve of her neck.

"I—I want to make love." The moment she said the words, she wanted to take them back. Not because she'd changed her mind, but because she'd said them wrong. Would they be making love or just satisfying a physical need? She sighed inwardly. Did it make any difference? If it did, then maybe she should get out of his bed and out of his life for good. "I want to have sex," she corrected.

"Are you sure?" Will murmured.

Jane crawled off the bed and stood beside it. He watched her as she grabbed the hem of her blouse and tugged it over her head without unbuttoning it. With trembling fingers, she reached for the button on her jeans but Will stopped her, sliding off the bed to stand beside her. Without a word, he dragged her into his embrace, his palms sliding over her naked skin.

Caught in an endless kiss, they began to undress each other, Jane growing bolder with each article of clothing tossed aside. She held her breath as he shoved her jeans down along her legs and helped her step out of them. As he stood, Jane let her fingers smooth along his arms to his hands. His body was more beautiful than she could have ever fantasized, long limbed and finely muscled, pure masculine symmetry. But his hands were perfection, his fingers long and tapered, eager to touch.

Drawing his hands up, she brought them to the clasp between her breasts. With deliberate care, he undid her bra and traced a path across her skin with his fingertips, circling the tight peaks of her nipples before gliding away. Jane suddenly felt light-headed, dizzy with arousal and tingling with anticipation. She fought to keep her eyes open, to watch him as his mouth trailed after his fingers, his lips hot on her skin.

Desperation began to set in and Jane grew impatient. A warm heat pooled between her legs, the ache growing with every fleeting caress. She found the waistband of his boxers and then the outline of his hard shaft and she gently wrapped her fingers around him. Will sucked in a sharp breath and, as if her touch had triggered something inside him, he quickly stripped them both of the last of their clothes and pulled her back down onto the bed.

He found the damp of her desire and he began to stroke her there. Jane writhed beneath him, stunned by the sensations that shot through her body. She'd never shared her release with a man but she knew she was so close with Will. When he slipped a finger inside her, she jerked, teetering near the edge. "Please," she cried, arching against his hand.

Every thought, every nerve in her body was focused on his touch. He was both her lover and her tormentor, pushing her closer to the edge, then drawing her back, forcing her to beg him for more. By the time he gave her the condom, she was frantic to feel him inside of her. She quickly sheathed him and pulled him on top of her.

But just as quickly, he rolled her over until she straddled his hips. Slowly Jane moved against him, sliding along his length, bringing herself closer to her own completion. He watched her as she moved, his eyes half-hooded with need, obviously fighting to resist his release as much as she tumbled toward hers.

And then suddenly, he shifted beneath her and he was inside her, first in sweet, shallow strokes, then thrusting deeper, driving into her, burying himself to the hilt. She matched his movements and when he slipped his fingers in between their bodies and touched her again, Jane cried out.

The orgasm ripped through her body, stealing her breath and stopping her heart. She convulsed around him as he increased his speed. A moment later, he joined her, murmuring her name as he climaxed.

For a long time, they lay together, neither one moving or speaking. And then he found her mouth and groaned softly against her lips. Jane sighed and smiled, completely sated and convinced that she'd never experience another man the way she'd experienced Will.

"You're beautiful," he murmured, smoothing her hair back from her face. "How is it that you're lying here in bed with me and not some other lucky guy?"

"I signed a contract six years ago," Jane said.

His smiled faded. "Is that the only reason?"

"I'm here because there's no other place I want to be," Jane said, dropping a kiss onto his lips. "I wanted you, Will, just as much as you wanted me. And the contract has nothing to do with that at all."

Satisfied with her answer, he pulled her against him, tucking her into the curve of his body, her backside nestled in his lap. Gently he ran his hands along her arms and then her thighs, as if he needed to reassure himself that she wasn't going to leave.

Jane closed her eyes and lost herself in his touch, knowing if he continued this lazy caress, she'd want him again. In truth, she'd never stopped wanting him. From the moment she'd first met Will, all those years ago, he had occupied a singular place in her heart, stealing a tiny bit of her soul every time he smiled at her.

And now, she'd surrendered, trading what little of her soul she had left for a night of passion. Somehow, lying here in his arms, Jane couldn't regret her decision. She'd finally found what she'd been missing in her life, a desire that completely overwhelmed her. And even if this was all they had, it would be enough for her—enough to know that for one special night, she'd loved Will McCaffrey and he'd loved her back.

WILL SLOWLY OPENED HIS EYES to the morning light filtering through his bedroom blinds. He sighed softly as his brain began to function and slowly, the memories of the previous night came into sharper focus. He reached out to the other side of the bed, hoping to find Jane curled up there, still asleep. But he wasn't surprised when he found her spot cold and empty.

He rolled onto his stomach and smiled sleepily. She may feel like sneaking out now, but Will was confident that wouldn't always be the case. After what they'd shared, he knew there would come a time, maybe in the very near future, maybe even tonight, when she'd choose to fall asleep *and* wake up in his arms.

Will grabbed her pillow and pulled it to his face, inhaling deeply. The scent of her brought a flood of memories racing into his mind. She'd been so careful, maintaining a cool distance whenever they were together. And then, a single instant had changed everything, the instant she'd asked him to kiss her again.

He replayed that kiss, wondering what it was that had caused her reserve to dissolve so quickly and thoroughly. One moment, she was flinching at his touch and the next she was melting in his arms. Will had always considered himself an expert in the wants and needs of women, but Jane was different. She didn't think like the women he'd known in the past and she certainly didn't act in any predictable way. First, she was distant and aloof, and then she was tearing at his shirt and touching him provocatively.

His response to her had been a complete surprise, not that she wasn't the sexiest woman he'd ever touched. With Jane, he'd felt something different, a connection that made their passion even more intense and his reactions even more fulfilling. She wasn't a virgin, that much was clear. And last night had been a long way from his first time. But yet, seduction had never felt so new and exciting as it had with her.

He'd forgotten all those others, forgotten the practiced art of making a woman need him, and he'd simply operated on instinct. Just a soft sigh or a simple look had told him all he needed to know, where Jane wanted to be touched and how. And all this had been driven by his own reactions.

At first, she had been almost unaware of the effect she had on him, of the level of desire that she could provoke with her touch. Her hands on his body had been hesitant, then growing more bold and determined, daring him to lose control. And in the end, she left him shuddering in his release, more certain than ever that this was a woman he couldn't live without.

"Oh, hell," Will muttered, rolling over on his back and throwing his arm over his eyes. What had begun as just a simple contract between friends had turned so complicated that even he couldn't untangle it—his feelings, her feelings, the motives that drew them together and the secrets that might tear them apart.

Jane didn't love him and that realization stung. For the first time in his life, he wanted a woman to fall head over heels, to look at him as if he were the only man in the universe. Yet every time Jane looked into his eyes, he saw doubt and indecision and apprehension—so acute that even his considerable charms couldn't soothe her fears.

Will cursed his decision to use the contract against her. Maybe if he'd just worked a little harder and worn her down, she might have accepted a date. And then another. And after a proper amount of time had passed, they might have decided to move in together. And then, marriage might have followed.

"Marriage," he said. A few months ago, the word had been enough to strike fear into his heart, yet now it seemed like a very appealing prospect. He could imagine himself married to Jane, building a life with her. The feelings growing inside him were strong enough to overwhelm his doubts about lifetime commitment. Will sighed. For the first time since his father had given his ultimatum, Will realized he may have been right. Getting serious about life could be a good thing.

The doorbell rang and Will frowned, wondering who would come by so early in the morning. He grabbed a pair of jeans and tugged them on, not bothering with his boxers, then shrugged into yesterday's shirt. As he dressed, he noticed Jane's clothes scattered on the floor. Will paused to pick up her lacy panties, fingering the soft fabric. He bunched them into his fist and jogged down the stairs.

Though he'd hoped to find Jane on the other side of the door, her mother greeted him instead with a chipper "good morning."

"Hello, Selma," Will said. "Jane has already gone to work."

Her expression fell. "She's avoiding me," Selma said, slipping inside the house. "I've been pushing her too hard." She sent Will an apologetic smile. "Sometimes I let my enthusiasm get the better of me."

Will reached out to shut the door, then noticed Jane's panties clutched in his hand. He quickly shoved them into his back pocket and followed Selma into the kitchen. She'd already found the coffeemaker and was filling the pot with cold water as he sat down at the breakfast bar.

"She's been really busy at work."

"Do you know if she plans to continue working after you're married?" Selma asked.

Will shrugged. "We haven't discussed that."

"Marriage takes a tremendous amount of time and commitment. Mr. Singleton and I are together today for only one reason. We worked very hard at our marriage. Don't get me wrong, marriage is a wonderful thing. It's like a garden, full of beautiful blooms and tantalizing scents. But it has its seasons, its good times and bad. And sometimes, the weeds and the bugs take over and you can't see the beauty anymore. You have to tend your garden, Will. You have to pull those weeds and spray those bugs. Do you understand what I'm saying?"

Will frowned. "I think I do."

"Don't get me wrong. I'm sure you two will be wonderful together. It's just taken her so long to get to this point in her life."

"Jane is only twenty-five," Will said. "It's not like she's an old maid."

"Thanks to you!" Selma said, patting him on the arm. "You've made her forget that awful boy from her past."

"What boy is that?"

"I don't know," Selma said. "Sometime during her first two years at Northwestern, she fell in love. But she never brought the boy home and she was very secretive about him. I think it might have been a case of un-requited love."

"She told you about this boy?" Will asked.

A faint blush colored Selma's cheeks. "No. I read about him in her journal. She left it out at Christmas and I took a little peek. I know, I'm probably a horrible mother, but she seemed so distant and preoccupied. I thought she might be on drugs or something."

"And what did you find out?" Will asked, his curiosity piqued.

"She always referred to him by his initials—P.C. But I'm sure you don't have to worry about him. This was years ago and Jane has probably forgotten him."

The thought of Jane madly in love with another man caused an unbidden surge of jealousy that Will didn't bother to ignore. "Right. You're right. After all, why would she have agreed to marry me if she was still car-rying a torch for this other guy?" Will stood up. "I re-ally have to get ready for work. I've got a meeting this morning and I—"

Selma held up her hand. "Say no more. I've got an appointment with the wedding planner. We're going to look at invitations. But there is one thing I'd like to ask before I leave." She gave him a serious look. "I'd appreciate it if you would use your influence with Jane to get her more involved in the wedding plans."

"I'll try," Will said as he walked with her to the front door. When he'd closed it behind Selma, he leaned back against it and raked his hand through his hair. He'd been uncertain about Jane's feelings from the start, but now he knew the reason. She'd lost the man she really loved. And now she had been forced to consider him—her second choice at best.

God, he'd lived just downstairs from her during that time period and he hadn't even known she was involved. But then, he'd been so embroiled in his own social life he hadn't had time to ask Jane about her own. Still, how could he have missed something as major as Jane falling in love?

Will cursed softly as he trudged up the stairs to his bedroom. Thurgood was curled up in front of the closet, sleeping soundly, while Will picked up the clothes scattered around the bedroom floor. He carefully folded Jane's things and set them on the end of the bed, then picked up his jacket and trousers and emptied the pockets.

His fingers closed around the velvet box and he pulled it out. It was probably a waste of money, buying the engagement ring while things were still so unsettled. But he'd chosen optimism over common sense, believing he'd finally found a woman worth loving.

Will sat down on the edge of the bed and slipped the ring onto the end of his index finger. The diamond flashed and glittered, as if taunting him with his stupidity. Maybe he ought to just give the ring to Jane, force her hand and see exactly how she felt. He had to believe there was something there after last night. Or had it been all about sex and nothing about love?

"Jeez, McCaffrey, this is poetic justice," he muttered. He'd spent his life in pursuit of no-strings sex and running hard from love and commitment. And now that he'd finally taken a step toward a real relationship, he was worried the woman he wanted was only interested in his body.

Maybe it was time to cut his losses and get out now. He'd rip up the contract and find out in short order if Jane really wanted to stay. But was he willing to take that chance? Maybe it was best to give her a little more time. After all, last night had signaled a major shift in their relationship. It could only get better from here.

Sighing deeply, Will tucked the ring back into the box and tossed it on his nightstand. He'd take it one day at a time. If—and when—the moment was right, Will would give her the diamond. And he'd damn well be sure she was going to accept it.

THE HOUSE WAS QUIET WHEN JANE got home from work. Thurgood barely lifted his head from his napping spot on the sofa as she entered. She'd been hoping for a little time to herself before she had to see Will, unsure of how they might be together after the previous night—and after she'd tiptoed out that morning without waking him.

She'd barely slept a wink, watching Will by the light of the city night. How many times had she fantasized about such a situation? Her fantasies had always been filled with romance, eloquent words and gallant gestures. But in reality, it had been all about passion—raw, uninhibited lust.

For the first time in her life, Jane had surrendered completely, allowing a man to take her places she'd been afraid to go in the past. Just the thought of what they'd done to each other brought a warm flush to her face. The way he'd touched and kissed her, the feel of him on top of her and inside her, sent a thrill racing through her body even now. There hadn't been pretty words or romantic declarations, but what they'd shared had forged a connection that couldn't be denied.

As she walked down the hall to her bedroom, Jane tugged her sweater over her head. The day had been exhausting, made even more so by her lack of sleep. She glanced at her watch, only to find it wasn't there. She'd taken it off last night in Will's room and had forgotten to grab it that morning. Jane guessed that she had at least an hour before Will got home. "A nap or a bath," she murmured.

Her bed looked so inviting that she decided on the nap. She stripped down to her underwear and pulled back the covers. But just as she was about to crawl in, she decided to retrieve her watch and the clothes she'd left in Will's room.

Dressed in just her underwear, Jane wandered across the hall and peeked inside the bedroom door. The bed was as they'd left it, the covers tangled and the sheets rumpled. She stared at it for a long moment, images of a naked and very aroused Will lingering in her mind. A tiny smile touched her lips and she crawled onto the bed and buried her face in his pillow.

Jane couldn't help but wonder when she'd spend the next night in his arms. Would it be assumed that they'd sleep together tonight? Falling into that pattern might be the natural progression in their relationship. Or it might just complicate matters between them.

She closed her eyes and let her thoughts drift, memories of Will filling her head—the feel of his skin beneath her hands, the sound of his voice as he murmured her name, the scent of his hair, damp at his nape. With a low moan, she rolled onto her stomach and reached out to search for her watch on the nightstand. But her hand came to rest on a small box.

She grabbed it, bracing herself on her elbows. Curious, Jane flipped it open, then gasped. Tucked into black velvet was a huge emerald-cut diamond in a simple platinum setting, the very same ring she'd pointed out at Bloomingdale's. With a quiet curse, she snapped the box shut and quickly put it back on the table. The urge to take a second look was overwhelming and Jane gave in to it.

"Oh, my," she murmured. The ring was exquisite, the diamond at least three or four carats and mounted in a simple setting. Though she'd chosen it capriciously, Jane had to admit that it was the most beautiful ring in the world. Instinct told her to close the box and leave the room, to forget about what she'd seen. But her discovery couldn't be ignored.

Was Will considering giving her this ring? Why buy it if he wasn't? And what would she say if he did offer it to her? Maybe it was simply to satisfy her original demand. "It's definitely showy," she said, slipping it on her ring finger. "Yes, we're engaged," she said to an invisible acquaintance. "And this is my fiancé, Will." Jane held her hand out in front of her, then sighed.

Even if he did offer it to her, there was no way she could accept. She yanked the ring off her finger and returned it and the box to the nightstand. Will had made his motivations clear. If his father hadn't been pressuring him, then he wouldn't even consider marriage. In

Will's mind, it was a good trade—his father's company for a wife. But Jane wanted to be more to him than just a means to an end. *She* wanted to be the prize worth winning, not his job promotion.

She couldn't trust him to love her and she couldn't allow herself to love him. "So why spend the next ten weeks together?" she muttered as she crawled off the bed. "Walk away now. Put some distance between you and him before it's too late."

Jane crossed the hall to her bedroom and tugged on a pair of jeans and a chenille sweater then wandered downstairs. She'd brought home some potting soil and decided she'd better get to repotting the plants Thurgood had attacked. Just as she'd finished and was cleaning up in the kitchen, she heard the back door open. Thurgood sat up, then leaped over the back of the sofa to greet Will. Jane felt her heart stop for a moment at seeing him. Though he was fully dressed in a suit and tie, she instantly saw the man who had made love to her last night.

"Hi," she murmured.

He glanced up and smiled at her. "Hi." Will's gaze fixed on hers as he crossed the family room into the kitchen and stood in front of her. He leaned close and brushed a kiss across her lips, cupping her cheek in his hand. "I missed you this morning."

"I had to be out to a job site early," Jane lied. "How was your day?"

"Long. From the time I got to the office, all I could think about was getting back home to you."

"Why is that?" Jane asked, turning to the refrigerator to retrieve a bottle of wine.

Will gently massaged her shoulders as he nuzzled her neck. "Do you have to ask?"

Jane closed her eyes and tipped her head back, losing herself for a moment in his touch. If she turned around, Jane knew he'd be there, ready to sweep her into another mind-altering kiss and that could only lead to his bedroom, and a repeat of last night's encounter. But she'd surrendered to her desire once. She couldn't let it happen again. "Would you like something to drink?" she asked, retreating a safe distance.

"Are you all right?" Will asked.

Jane poured herself a glass of wine and took a long sip. "I'm fine. I was just thinking about—"

"Us?" Will asked.

"No, the holidays." She grabbed a magazine from the counter and flipped through it, grateful for something to distract her attention. "Things have been a little slow at work and I think I'd like to take a little vacation over Thanksgiving. And maybe Christmas, too."

"A vacation would be great," Will said, his expression brightening. "We could get away to someplace warm. Where would you like to go? Hawaii would be nice this time of year."

"Actually, I was thinking about going alone. I thought you might like some time to yourself." She risked a glance up, only to find a wary expression on his handsome face.

"Jane, if I wanted to spend time by myself, I wouldn't have asked you to move in with me. I think if you're going to go on vacation, then we should go together, after the holidays."

She shrugged. "It was just an idea. I thought if I was out of town, then I wouldn't have to deal with my mother. She's going to want to make a big production of the holidays now that she thinks we're engaged. I'm afraid she might try to throw us a party."

Will sighed and distractedly ran his thumb over the back of her hand. "I was hoping maybe we could have your family and my family here for Thanksgiving dinner," he said. "It will give them a chance to meet and get to know each other."

Jane sent him a sideways glance, the suggestion causing her to laugh out loud. "You've got to be kidding."

"I'm not," he said.

"Do you have any idea the kind of work that goes into preparing a meal like that? Days of planning and shopping and cooking. It doesn't just pop out of the kitchen fully cooked and ready to serve."

"I can help," Will said. "I just think it would be good to get our families together and Thanksgiving seems like a logical choice. And it wouldn't have to be a big deal. Your parents, my father, my sister and her husband and three children. With you and me, that's only ten people."

"Why are you so set on this?"

"And if you don't want to cook, we can have it catered."

"You can't cater a Thanksgiving dinner. It's just not right."

"You can't?" Will asked, his expression falling.

Jane stared at him for a long moment, an uneasy feeling growing in her stomach. "Will, what did you do?"

"Your mother talked to my father about Thanksgiving. She invited our family to your family's place, but my father wanted to have Thanksgiving at our family home and it was about to turn into a big argument. So I invited my family and your family to have Thanksgiving here," he said, wincing, "in our house."

Jane groaned. "No. No, no, no. You can't do this! I thought you'd learned your lesson after you invited my mother and her wedding planner for a visit."

"I didn't invite her, she invited herself. Come on, Jane. This is all part of learning more about each other, don't you think? We have to see how we handle stressful situations and the holidays are stressful."

"Well, I'm sure we'll get enough of that in the next hour while we're having a blistering argument about how fiancés or husbands or even moderately considerate boyfriends don't just invite ten people for the holidays without discussing it with their significant other!"

"Do we have to have an argument? Can't you just yell at me for a little longer and then we can kiss and make up?"

"Don't try that charm on me, mister," Jane warned, shaking her finger at him. "It's not going to work."

"It worked pretty well last night," Will said, slipping his arms around her waist. "So go ahead. Rip me a new one. I'm ready."

Jane sighed. Why did she even try to fight him? She was lost before she even began. All he had to do was touch her and her anger dissolved. The only defense she had was to keep her distance, to stay just out of reach of his hands and his lips. "Well, if we're having

Thanksgiving dinner here, I have a lot of work to do. You don't have pots and pans, you don't have china or crystal or even a tablecloth and napkins. Will, you don't even have a decent dining room table. Where are we going to feed all these people?"

"We could have one of those, what do you call them, buffets? Right. We could have a buffet."

Just the thought of ten people standing around the kitchen with paper plates and plastic forks caused a hysterical giggle to slip from her throat. If she wanted to prove to Will what a horrible wife she'd make, she'd have the perfect opportunity on Thanksgiving Day.

But was she ready to give up on him? Or was there a part of her that still believed he was and always would be the perfect man for her?

6

WILL DROVE THE LAST SCREW into the bracket then carefully hung the curtain rod over the window. He stepped back and looked at it critically. It was a tiny bit crooked, but once Jane did whatever she planned to do, no one would be able to tell.

He flipped the power drill in his hand like a six-shooter and grinned. "I'm good. I can do the handyman thing."

Over the past week, Jane had turned into a woman obsessed, spending her days shopping and her evenings turning his house into a warm and inviting home—a place where he hoped she planned to stay. She'd thrown out every last bit of pink and brought in colors and accents that reflected her love of the outdoors.

In truth, Will liked the new decor. It wasn't a bit fussy or feminine, just simple and comfortable. She'd added soft throw pillows to the leather sofas in the living room and family room, she'd bought some new lamps, but her big purchase had been a huge dining-room table to replace the small square table that he'd always used.

But it was the nights that had made his Thanksgiving faux pas so worthwhile. All the tension she built up during the day had to find a release, and she found it in bed with him, caught up in a maelstrom of passion that grew more wild and uninhibited with every night they spent together.

She still hadn't dropped the last bit of her reserve, though. Every night, they began in separate bedrooms. Then sooner or later, one of them would give in and silently appear at the other's bedroom door. Sometimes they slept in her bed and sometimes in his. But to Will's delight, she always woke up in his arms.

He glanced at his watch, then set the drill on the table and walked out the front door. He found Jane where he'd left her a half hour ago, working on the small garden between the sidewalk and the house. Will walked down the front steps and squatted beside her as she furiously dug at the dirt.

"What are you going to plant?" he asked, his gaze fixing on her nape where a sheen of perspiration had dampened her hair. He fought the urge to press his mouth to the spot, to inhale the scent of her hair and lose himself again in thoughts of her body naked in his arms.

"These mums," she said, holding up a pot. "Just to brighten things up for Thanksgiving."

Will took the pot from her, his fingers brushing against hers. A memory flashed in his mind, those fingers closing around him, driving him to the edge of passion then retreating. He cleared his throat as he pushed the image aside. "Isn't this the wrong time of year to plant flowers?"

She shook her head. "Mums are hardy. They can stand a light freeze. And the weather isn't supposed to get cold for another week." Jane patted the dirt around the last of the flowers, then sat back on her heels and tugged off her gardening gloves. "What do you think?"

"Very pretty," he murmured, referring to the rosy color in her cheeks and the winsome smile on her lips. There wasn't a flower on the planet that held a candle to Jane's beauty. He picked up a paper bag from the sidewalk. "What are these?"

"Daffodil bulbs. I planted a bunch of those, too. They'll bloom in the spring, sometime in April."

Will picked up one of the bulbs and turned it over in his hand. She was planting flowers for the spring even though she wasn't sure she'd be living with him in the spring. He wanted to take that as a hopeful sign, but Will knew better. Her feelings about him seemed to change with the sun rising and setting.

During the day, she barely acknowledged that they were lovers. He felt an almost pathological need to test her, to touch her and kiss her, to reassure himself that he hadn't imagined their nights together. They had passion, but he wanted more. He wanted to know she felt something for him, that the feelings growing in his heart were reflected in hers.

"It's getting chilly out here," Will said, rubbing her upper arms. "I made a fire inside. Why don't you come in and I'll make you some dinner?" He stood up and held out his hands to her, then pulled her to her feet.

He stared down at her as the breeze ruffled her dark hair. Will smoothed his palm over her cheek. "You look tired," he said. "I'm sorry if this was too much. I can always call and tell everyone that we've decided to leave town for Thanksgiving."

"It's four days away," Jane said, shaking the dirt out of her gloves. "Besides, my mother would never get over it. It would be a major breech in social etiquette to cancel at this late date. And she's just dying to meet your family." She picked up her gardening tools and Will took them from her. "I have to pick up wine-glasses and then I have to stop at the store and order the turkey. And I've got a bunch of recipes to go through so I can make my grocery list and—"

Will groaned, then dragged her into his arms and stopped her "to-do" list with a kiss. His mouth was hot on hers and he gently parted her lips with his tongue, anxious to taste her. When he pulled back, he found her looking up at him, her eyes wide, as if the kiss had surprised her. "Why are you doing this?" he asked.

"Kissing you?"

"No. Doing all this work for Thanksgiving."

"I—I want to make the holiday nice," she said. "If you're going to do something, you might as well do it right, that's what my mother always says." She smiled ruefully. "God, I'm turning into my mother, aren't I?"

Will closed his eyes and pressed his lips to her fore-head. "You're nothing like your mother. And you don't have to prove anything to me, Janie. I know how you feel. If it weren't for this agreement we have, you'd be spending Thanksgiving somewhere else." He brushed a strand of hair off her cheek. "Do you re-member those dinners you used to make for me back in law school? I always loved coming to your place."

"That's because you never had any food in your refrigerator," Jane teased. "If I didn't feed you, who would?"

"I didn't always come for the food. Your apartment was always so warm and inviting. I felt comfortable there." He took her hand and wove his fingers through hers. "Even though the food was good, most times I came just because I wanted to be with you."

"You did?" she asked, her voice soft and breathy.

He took her hand and drew it up to his lips, kissing her fingertips one by one. "You were a really good cook back then. But you were a better friend. And I'm not sure I realized until now how important that was to me."

Jane stared at her fingers as he kissed each one again, an uneasy expression on her pretty face. "We should really go inside," she murmured. "It is getting cold out here."

For a fleeting instant, Will thought he saw desire flare in her eyes. But then it was gone, replaced by a mask of indifference. What was she scared of? Why couldn't she seem to surrender that last little bit of herself to him? "All right," he conceded. "I have to get working on dinner. I was thinking of whipping up a batch of liver."

Jane giggled, her smile warming him as if the sun had suddenly appeared from behind the clouds. "I'm willing to concede that my housewife-from-hell tactics didn't work. I think I could have fed you Alpo and you would have asked for seconds." They walked into the house and when they reached the kitchen, Jane grabbed a bottle of water from the refrigerator. "So, if you didn't like the food, why didn't you speak up?"

Will slipped his arms around her waist and trapped her against the edge of the counter. "I got to sit across the dinner table from you, what could I possibly have to complain about?"

"You have to stop saying things like that," Jane said, twisting out of his embrace. "I might just fall for you."

"Would that be so bad? Besides, I'm being honest. I like having you here, Janie. I like seeing you in my house, cooking in my kitchen, digging in my garden, watching my television."

A pretty blush stained her cheeks, but Will suspected she didn't believe a word he said. He'd always considered himself an expert with the ladies, always knowing what to say to make them want him. But Jane was different. She seemed to see right inside of him, past the charm and the smiles and the clever come-ons, right into the deepest corners of his soul.

"I should really make my shopping list," she said.

"You should stop changing the subject every time I try to talk about us," Will said.

Jane sighed. "Why do we have to talk about us? It is what it is, Will." Her tone was laced with impatience.

"That's fine. But I don't know what it is. One minute I feel like you're here with me and the next you've checked out. You run hot and cold and I never know what to expect."

"If you don't like it, then tell me to leave," Jane said, her voice now filled with icy anger.

"That's not what I want, Janie. I just want you to give this your best effort." He took her hands but she snatched them away.

"Do you want me to pretend that I feel something I don't?" she asked.

"Do you have to pretend with me?" Will countered, his gaze meeting hers and holding it. "I don't see any pretending when you're in my arms at night, when I'm moving inside of you. Are you pretending then?"

Instead of answering, she looked away. "No," she finally said.

"And how does that make you feel? We're so good together, Janie. Not just good, incredible. And it's all I can do to keep from dragging you upstairs right now and proving it all over again."

"I—I don't know what you want me to say. That's just sex. What you're asking for is love. And though your charm may have lured my body into your bed, it doesn't have any effect on my heart."

Will stared at her, her words cutting to the quick. "God, you must have loved him very much to still be carrying such a huge torch."

Jane blinked, then frowned in confusion. "What are you talking about? What torch?"

"The guy. P.C. The one you loved in college? He must have been quite the guy."

A gasp burst from her lips. "How do you know about P.C.?"

"It doesn't matter. All that matters is that he's in the past and you have to get on with your future. Carrying a torch for a guy you can't have is only going to close you off to the possibilities of a guy you *could* have."

"How do you know about him?" Jane repeated.

"Your mother told me you were in love with someone you met while you were at Northwestern and that you've never really gotten over him."

"And how did she know this?" Jane groaned. "Of course I know. She read my journals. I have the nosiest mother on the planet. I should have known she wouldn't stop looking for them until she found them."

"It doesn't really make a difference how she found out. That's not the point. The point is he's not here and I am. So it's time you forgot about the past and moved on."

Jane slowly shook her head. "Well, when you and my mother figure out a way to make me forget that boy I knew, you let me know. Because it's not so easy. In truth, I'd like to forget all about him—but I can't." With that, she turned on her heel and walked away.

Will watched her walk through the family room and out the back door. He cursed softly as he heard her start the truck and pull out of the garage. "How the hell am I supposed to make this work?" he muttered. How could he compete with the memory of a perfect relationship?

He'd damn well better figure out a way! He was fast falling in love with Jane Singleton and he wasn't about to lose her to some paragon of manhood from her past. He'd need to show her exactly what she'd be missing if she walked away, what he could give her that no other man could. As long as Jane was living in his house, he was going to take every opportunity to make his case.

She may have loved someone else in the past, but he was here, in the present, and that had to count for something.

JANE OPENED THE FRONT DOOR of the small Wicker Park office building. She'd passed the office hundreds of times on her way to and from work, yet only recently noticed the Free Consultation sign in the window. So she'd stopped in that morning to make an appointment and had been told to come back in three hours. Attorney Andrea Schaefer, specialist in family law, would be the answer to all her problems.

Or would she? The more time she spent with Will, the harder it was to imagine life without him. He'd completely swept her off her feet, the same way he had when they'd met eight years ago. And as if the past was destined to repeat itself, she was falling in love with him all over again.

A tiny smile quirked the corners of her mouth as she thought back to the previous night's conversation. Will had somehow been convinced there had been another man in her life. She'd seen the spark of jealousy in his eyes and took a perverse delight in the fact that the man she'd loved had been him. P.C. had been code for Prince Charming, her secret nickname for Will.

Still, nothing that Will said had altered her feelings for him. Yes, he was charming and sexy and downright irresistible. But he was still the man she knew in college, a man who'd never been able to commit to a woman in his life. To him, Jane was a prize, dangling just out of his reach. And once he had her, the novelty would wear off and he'd toss her aside.

Jane drew a deep breath and opened the door to the office suite. The pretty young receptionist smiled at her as she stepped inside, recognizing Jane from her earlier visit. "Hello, Miss Singleton."

"Hi," Jane said, returning her smile.

"Ms. Schaefer is waiting for you. You can go right back. It's the middle door."

Jane nodded and walked toward the center office. Before she reached the door, a tall blonde stepped out. She wore a wildly patterned skirt, a funky sweater and trendy pumps, not at all the typical lawyer outfit. Her curly hair was twisted in a knot and fastened haphazardly at her nape. "Hi, Jane, I'm Andrea Schaefer. Come on in and take a seat."

When Jane was settled in a chair on the other side of Andrea's desk, the lawyer sat down across from her. "You say you have a contract dispute. Did you bring a copy of the contract?"

Jane nodded and handed her the photocopy of the single-page document.

As Andrea skimmed it, her expression turned from casual interest to mild amusement. "This is a marriage contract. I don't believe I've ever seen one of these."

"I signed the contract six years ago. It was really stupid, I know, but I thought it was just a joke. I never thought he'd try to enforce it."

"Did this man give you anything?"

Jane blinked, wondering how she was supposed to answer such a personal question. Was the fact that they already consummated the marriage really that important? Yes, Will gave her undeniable pleasure in bed and orgasms that made her toes curl. Though she enjoyed attorney-client privilege, that didn't mean her lawyer couldn't tell her she was an idiot for sleeping with Will. "Well, I guess...I mean, we really give to each other…the sex is good. Really good. Does that make a difference?"

Andrea chuckled. "I wasn't talking about sex. Did he give you consideration? Maybe money or an expensive gift?"

Her thoughts jumped to the ring she'd found in his room. "You think he should pay me for sex?" Jane asked.

"No, I'm talking about when you signed the contract six years ago. What did he give you in return for you agreeing to marry him?"

"I don't think he gave me anything," Jane said, frowning. "He had a bouquet of flowers—English roses, which are my favorites, and—" She tried to remember the events of that night. All she'd ever wanted to remember was the kiss they'd shared. Everything else had faded in comparison. "Wait, he did give me something. He gave me five dollars. I thought it was strange but he said it was important. I told him I'd use it for laundry money, but I tucked it away in one of my journals. I probably still have it."

"That payment is important. It's called consideration. This man obviously knew what he was doing."

"He was a law student at Northwestern."

"So was I. And one of the first cases we learned in our contracts course as freshmen was Wood versus Lady Duff Gordon, New York, 1917, I think. Wood gave Lady Duff an engagement ring, she agreed to marry him, and consideration makes the contract valid. At the time, the judge ruled that she had to marry the guy."

"So because Will gave me five dollars, I have to marry him?"

A pensive expression crossed Andrea's face and she skimmed the contract again. "Essentially, the contract is legal," she said distractedly. "Although I don't think it would hold up in court, even with consideration paid. There's not a judge who's going to force you to marry someone you don't want to marry. But if this guy pressed his case, you'd have to hire a lawyer and settle." She stopped suddenly. "Oh my God. I can't believe this. Will McCaffrey? Northwestern Law, class of '98?"

"Yes."

Andrea chuckled and shook her head. "I'm afraid I might have a conflict of interest here. I know Will. He graduated a year ahead of me at Northwestern Law." She paused. "We had a few classes together and I used to have this huge crush on him. Almost every girl in law school did. We even went out once."

Jane stared at the lawyer. Was this what she'd face all over Chicago? She knew Will had dated a lot of women from law school, but this was too much of a coincidence!

"How is Will?" Andrea asked. "Things must not be too good if he has to call in a contract to get a wife. What happened? Did he go bald? Get a little paunchy?"

Jane shook her head. "No, he looks pretty much the same as he did in law school. Maybe even a little more handsome...I guess polished would be a better word."

"Oh," Andrea said the word coming out on a sigh. "Will McCaffrey, a little more polished. God, he must be gorgeous then. That man was just too charming for his own good."

"Yeah, he pretty much still is," Jane admitted with a weak smile.

"So why don't you want to marry him? You don't love him?"

"No," Jane said. "Yes." She stared at her fingers, twisted together in her lap. "Maybe I do. A little. Or maybe I'm just swept away by his charm. He makes me forget the man he really is and makes me believe he can be the man I want. And whenever we're together, I feel as if I'm the only woman in the world who can make him happy."

"And how do you think he feels about you?"

"I think he likes me. I also think he needs to get married and that has a lot to do with how he feels."

"And if you called his bluff on this and told him you were going to marry him, what do think he'd do?"

"I tried that already. And I think he's prepared to marry me—but not for any of the right reasons. Will is used to getting what he wants, especially when it comes to women. I'd have to pay for a lawyer to fight the contract and he wouldn't. I have no money and he does."

"Well, if you want to marry him, Jane, I'd advise you to sit tight and see what happens. If you don't want to marry him, then call him on this. The worst he can do is take you to court. My guess is that he's not going to do that. He's a smart lawyer and he's got to know that his chances in court aren't good."

"So the decision is all mine?"

"It is. And if you need my help, feel free to call," Andrea said, pushing up from her desk. "But I'm pretty sure you can solve this problem on your own."

Jane shook Andrea's hand, murmuring her thanks, then left the office, amazed that all her problems had been solved in less than five minutes. But even though she had answers, she wasn't sure about her decision. She could walk out of Will's house today and never look back and he'd probably let her go. But did she really want to leave? Was she willing to write him off so quickly? Or did she still harbor a secret fantasy that she and Will were destined to be together?

Six years ago, Jane had been certain she knew everything there was to know about Will. He was an accomplished flirt and an unrepentant ladies' man. He was charming and attentive, but avoided commitment at every turn. Women had a special place in his life—on his arm or in his bed—but only until he got bored and moved on.

In the end, she'd counted herself lucky that nothing had ever happened between them. But maybe it might have been better if it had. They could have slept together, he could have dumped her, and she could have hated him for the rest of her life. Instead she had lived for six years with these unresolved feelings, allowing him to plague her dreams and taint every relationship she'd ever had with a man.

Each potential boyfriend or lover had been held up against the Will McCaffrey standard and ultimately, found lacking. But now she had Will, not exactly the way she wanted him, but she still had him. She could marry him but she'd have to learn to live with the fact that he didn't really love her, that she'd merely been a convenient means to an end. Or she could walk away now and save her heart and her soul from the inevitable shattering end to their relationship.

Maybe there had been a time when she could have settled for less than perfect with him. But not anymore. She deserved to be loved and appreciated and cherished and Jane was not going to consider marriage until she found a man who would give her exactly that. From everything she remembered about Will, he wasn't that man.

Jane walked down Damen Avenue toward the spot where she'd parked the pickup truck. What had ever possessed her to accept his offer? Yes, she'd been worried about money, but she could have slept on Lisa's sofa or gone home to her parents' house. Instead she'd fallen into the same old trap, hoping that maybe this time, Will would be the man she'd always wanted him to be.

When she reached the truck, she hopped inside but didn't put the key in the ignition. Instead she stared out the windshield. He'd been so sweet and so considerate. And their nights had been more than she'd ever dreamed possible. Maybe he had changed and left his playboy ways behind him.

"No!" she muttered, shaking her head. The plain and simple fact was that guys like Will didn't change. Besides, he had forced her into this agreement. He'd done all but threaten to take her to court. And if she hadn't been in such financial trouble, she might have turned him down on the spot. He didn't love her. He just needed her to get what he wanted.

"So I'll leave," she said, starting the truck.

She had twelve people to feed for Thanksgiving after adding Lisa and Roy to the guest list. She had a couple hundred dollars worth of groceries in the cupboards and a turkey thawing in the refrigerator. Once the last guest left, she'd sit down with Will and tell him she wanted out.

And then, she'd finally get on with the rest of her life.

"WHAT TIME IS IT?"

Will glanced over at Jane, watching her reflection in the wide bathroom mirror. "It's two minutes later than the last time you asked," he said. "You have plenty of time. They're not supposed to be here for at least another fifteen or twenty minutes."

"How am I supposed to get ready with you hovering over me like this?"

"I'm not hovering," he murmured, tipping his head to the side and pulling the razor over his cheek. "I'm shaving." She'd been edgy all morning and he'd tried to tease her out of her black mood, but to no avail. "We can always call this off," he said as he rinsed the razor. "When they get to the door, I'll just tell them to go away."

This brought a tiny smile to her lips. "You'd do that?"

"I'd do anything to make you smile," he said, giving her his most flirtatious grin.

She rolled her eyes, then picked up a tube of lipstick. Will gently took it from her fingers. "You don't need this stuff. You're beautiful just the way you are."

Jane snatched it back from him and set it on the vanity top. "You're trying to flatter me out of my bad mood, aren't you?"

He slipped his arms around her waist and drew her closer. "No, I have ulterior motives."

She grabbed the towel from around his shoulders and dabbed at the bits of shaving cream left on his face. "And what motives are those?" she asked.

Will grabbed the lipstick again and closed it in his fist. "When I kiss you, I don't want anything coming between us, especially lipstick."

"And do you want to kiss me right now?" Jane asked, her voice wavering slightly, her gaze fixed on his lips.

"Sweetheart, I want to kiss you all the time." With that, Will gently lifted her up onto the edge of the vanity. He furrowed his fingers through her hair and captured her mouth. To his relief, Jane's usual indifference dissolved the moment his lips touched hers. Her hands smoothed over his bare chest, pushing his shirt aside.

Over the past few days, he'd come to the conclusion that he couldn't live without Jane. The revelation had hit him hard. When he'd decided to use the contract against her, he'd never intended to fall in love. But now that he had, he was at a loss as to what to do. How could he reveal his growing feelings without scaring her away? And how could he make her feel about him the way he felt about her?

Will nuzzled her neck then unbuttoned her silk blouse and trailed kisses over her shoulder. The scent of her was intoxicating, making his head spin with every breath he took. He pulled her thighs up against his hips, her skirt bunching, revealing the full length of

her bare legs. His palms skimmed down to her ankles
and back up again, as he probed the damp recesses of
her mouth.

Jane braced her hands behind her and leaned back,
her blouse falling open. "We shouldn't do this," she
murmured. "We don't have—"

His hands slipped beneath her skirt and he hooked
his fingers over her panties. Slowly he tugged them
down, past her knees and over her ankles.

"Time," she finished.

"We have plenty of time." Will slowly slid his hand
between her thighs and when he reached the damp
juncture, he began to stroke her gently. Jane's breath
caught in her throat and she moaned, arching against
his fingers.

Why was it so simple to possess her body, yet im-
possible to capture her heart? Even as he seduced her,
Will suspected that she'd somehow managed to detach
the two. When he kissed her and caressed her, there
was always a corner of her heart or a piece of her soul
he couldn't touch.

"Tell me you want me to stop," he murmured, bend-
ing down to press a kiss on the inside of her thigh. His
fingers slipped inside her and another moan tore from
her throat. "Tell me, Janie. I'll stop if you want me to."

"No," she said, breathless. "Don't stop."

With a low growl, Will grabbed her waist and pulled
her closer to the edge of the vanity, shoving her skirt
up around her hips. He bent down and continued his
gentle assault, this time taking her with his mouth and
his tongue.

He listened as her breathing quickened and her body

tensed. As he brought her closer to her climax, Will felt himself grow hard with desire. But he focused on Jane's pleasure, taking delight in the tiny sighs and whispered pleas that always preceded her release. Though he couldn't possess her heart, Will knew he'd conquered her body. He knew exactly how to pleasure her, how to make her ache and shudder. But his need to possess her had turned to an obsession. He'd become determined to prove he was the right man for her, bent on driving every memory of that other man from her head. When she remembered desire and passion and earth-shattering release, she would see his face and no other.

Jane shifted above him and Will looked up at her. Her eyes were closed and her bottom lip was caught between her teeth as if that were the only thing holding her back, that tiny bit of pain she inflicted on herself. He plunged his tongue inside her and she cried out, her hands frantically furrowing through his hair, drawing him closer, ready for her release.

Just then, the doorbell rang. Jane's eyes flew open and her body stiffened. She looked at Will through a haze, as if she'd somehow lost herself in the sensations, forgetting who they were and what they were doing. She reached down to push her skirt back into place, but Will brushed her hands away.

"Let me finish," he murmured.

"They're at the door," Jane said.

"They can wait."

"No. No, they can't." Grasping his shoulders, she shoved him back and hopped off the vanity.

Will sat back on his heels and watched as she restored order to her clothes, slipping back into her panties, then raking her trembling fingers through her hair. He wanted to reach out and touch her again, take her that last little way to her orgasm. But even he could see there was no going back now. "We'll continue this later," he said, levering to his feet.

She looked at him, her gaze meeting his for an intense moment. Then she shook her head and hurried out of the bathroom. Will braced his hands on the edge of the vanity and stared at his reflection in the mirror. "What the hell are you doing?" he muttered. "You can't force her to love you. If it isn't there, you have to let her go."

Will tugged his shirt back over his shoulders and buttoned it, then quickly shoved the tails into his trousers. He ignored the erection that their encounter had caused but took a moment to splash cold water over his face. As he strode back to his bedroom to retrieve his sport coat and loafers, he cursed himself roundly. Though this little interlude had been enjoyable, Will knew he'd be able to think of nothing else for the rest of the afternoon—except maybe continuing where he'd left off once all the guests had gone home.

By the time he'd reached the bottom of the stairs, his desire had abated. Jane had opened the front door and her parents stood on the stoop next to Will's father. From the expressions on their faces, they'd already met before they'd even stepped in and it hadn't gone well. Selma was already in tears.

Jane ushered them inside, then sent Will a shaky smile, her cheeks still flushed and her hair tousled.

"Would you like to make the introductions?" she asked.

Selma ignored her daughter and continued on with a conversation started outside. "I'm just saying that you're going to have to put a limit on the number of guests you invite. The reception room can only hold three hundred and I have two-fifty on our list."

Will's father sent his son an aggravated look, then turned to Jane. Will quickly jumped in with the introductions and Jim McCaffrey firmly shook Jane's hand before he followed Selma into the living room. "I have business associates and family and friends to invite. Fifty is just not enough. Now, I'd suggest you find a larger room for the reception. If it's a matter of money, then—"

"It is certainly not a matter of money," Selma said. "But this room is perfect. It's large but very intimate. I've always dreamed Jane would have her reception at our country club."

Jane leaned closer to Will. "You have to keep my mother from talking about the wedding," she murmured. "Get in there and change the subject!"

Will brushed a quick kiss across her cheek and whispered back, "And while I'm at it, I'll just send in my application for sainthood because after I do that, I'll have the required miracle."

Flustered, Jane kissed her father, then hurried off to the kitchen. Jane's father chuckled and held out his hand to Will. "Hello, Will. Edward Singleton. It's a pleasure to finally meet you."

Will shook his hand and smiled warmly. "It's a pleasure to meet you, sir."

"Call me Edward. So, where can a guy get a drink here? I've been listening to this wedding talk for days now and I'm starting to get this pain in my backside that only a good glass of Scotch can ease."

"I have some single malt. Let me get you some."

"That sounds good," Edward said.

They left Selma and Jim arguing over square footage and table size and dance bands. "Mrs. Singleton certainly is excited about this wedding," Will commented as they strolled into the dining room. They stopped at the table and Edward looked at the festive setting that Jane had laid out.

"I've been married to that woman for nearly thirty years and I still don't understand her. She throws herself into her projects and won't accept anything less than perfection. And this wedding, she's been looking forward to this since Jane was born." He shook his head. "I love her, mind you, but I don't understand her. Tell me something, do you understand Jane?"

"Not completely," Will said. "I don't always know what she's thinking. But maybe that's a good thing."

"Do you love her?"

Will hadn't been expecting the question, but felt compelled to answer. "I do," he said, realizing that his words were the absolute truth. "I've never been in love before, but I'm pretty sure this is how it's supposed to feel."

Edward chuckled. "And how is that?"

"Confusing. Frustrating. Completely out of control, but in a good way. I do know that all I want is for Jane to be happy. And I think I can give her that."

"I hope you can," Edward said. "Because if you hurt

my little girl, I'll hunt you down and break every bone in your body."

Will forced a smile, but as he looked into Edward Singleton's eyes, he saw that the man was dead serious. "I'll keep that in mind," he murmured.

7

JANE PULLED OPEN THE DOOR of the oven and carefully lifted out the turkey, setting the pan next to the sink. She'd fussed over the turkey for the past two hours, basting it carefully, turning it so it would brown evenly and watching the thermometer until it reached the correct temperature. And finally, it was the epitome of poultry perfection—which was saying a lot considering the rest of the day was falling apart at the seams.

Jane's mother and Will's father had barely said a civil word to each other since they'd arrived and after a few glasses of wine, the atmosphere had turned tense and emotional. When they weren't in the midst of a heated discussion about the wedding, Jane's mother was closed in the bathroom weeping and Will's father was standing in a corner glowering. Selma no doubt had anticipated a much smoother introduction to Will's family, one where his father agreed with everything she had to say.

In truth, Jane wasn't really sure why Jim McCaffrey was acting like such an ass. She suspected that after meeting her and her parents, he was having second thoughts about his son marrying into the Singleton family. Jane had decided not to get in the middle of the conflict and instead, busied herself in the kitchen. Lisa and Roy had arrived shortly after Will's sister and her family, and they'd volunteered to help her with dinner preparations, while Will did his best to entertain his two nieces and his nephew with video games and Thurgood's dog tricks. Melanie and Ronald were getting acquainted with Jane's father.

Jane maneuvered the turkey onto a platter, then set the pan on the stove to make gravy. As she stirred water and wine into the drippings, she glanced up at the clock, silently calculating. The meal would take at least an hour and if she was lucky, they'd all be gone a half hour after that. "4:00 p.m. at the latest."

"Everything looks so good," Lisa said in a cheerful voice.

Jane continued to stir the gravy, the steam rising and curling her hair. "Thank God, you're here. I don't know what I would have done without you. This is just too much—the food, the family, the fighting. I can't believe my mother was arguing with Will's dad. She hates conflict."

"Your mother is a lot tougher than you give her credit for. Besides, she wants what's best for her daughter—a perfect wedding."

"I'm going to have to tell her sooner or later that there isn't going to be a wedding. It's going to break her heart."

"Maybe not. I don't think she's looking forward to another holiday with Will's family. Maybe she'll be relieved." Lisa wiped her hands on a dish towel. "And who knows, maybe there will be a wedding." She grinned when Jane sent her a dark look. "I've filled the water glasses. What's next?"

"Grab that sieve and hold it over that saucepan. If I serve lumpy gravy, my mother will be horrified. She taught me how to make gravy when I was six."

"You know, I'm really impressed," Lisa said, watching as Jane strained the gravy. "For a girl who is trying hard not to be the perfect wife, I'd say you're approaching June Cleaver status. So what do you have planned? Is the turkey half raw? Or maybe you put too much salt in the dressing? One time my mother left the package of giblets inside the turkey and pulled it out at the table with a spoonful of stuffing. That really impressed the guests."

"I'm doing this straight," Jane said.

"Why?"

"Because Will figured out my little scheme and called me on it. And if I don't do this up right, my mother will blame herself. I just want to get through the rest of the day without her bursting into tears again." Jane brushed an errant strand of hair from her forehead. "If the salads are on the table we can start. Get everyone seated and put my mother and Will's father at opposite ends of the table."

Lisa stepped up beside her and slipped her arm around Jane's shoulders. "You're doing great. Never mind that you look like you've been run over by a bus."

At this point in the day, Jane was simply happy to maintain her composure, much less portray the perky hostess. "I want you to promise once everyone has finished their pumpkin pie, you'll get up and go home— and take them all with you. Now promise me."

Lisa giggled. "I may have been wrong. June Cleaver

you're not. Where is that apron of yours? Maybe if you put that on your mood will improve." She grabbed Roy and pushed him in the direction of the family room. "Honey, why don't you tell Will, Melanie, Ronald and the kids that dinner is about to be served? I'll go inform the Bickersons."

A few moments later, the children ran through the kitchen. Will wandered behind them and stood next to Jane at the counter. He slipped his arms around her waist. "What do you want me to do?" he asked.

"Shoot me," Jane said. "Put me out of my misery."

"Not a chance."

"This is your fault. If you hadn't invited them, I wouldn't be going through hell right now. I'd be lying on a beach in Florida working on my tan and drinking Mai Tais."

"Janie, everything is wonderful. The table looks beautiful and if the food tastes anywhere near as good as it smells, it will be out of this world. If they can't appreciate everything you've done, then I plan to serve them a mighty big piece of my mind before I serve them any turkey."

"Please," Jane begged, "don't start another argument. I just want to get through dinner with smiling faces and pleasant conversation. I don't care if they hate the food, as long as they don't hate each other by the end of the meal."

Will leaned forward and kissed her forehead, smoothing his hand through her hair. "I promise I'll make this up to you. I'll be your slave for the next week. I'll fan your face and feed you bonbons and massage your feet. Anything you ask, I'll do."

Jane thought about all the things he'd done to her in the bathroom earlier that afternoon. Her first impulse was to ask to him to finish what he'd started, but she pushed the thought aside. After all, she was supposed to be ending it with him after this fiasco was over, wasn't she? "I'd be happy if you did the dishes."

"It's the least I can do. Now, do you want me to take the turkey in?"

"Leave it here. It has to rest before you carve it."

He took her hand and tucked it in the crook of his arm. "Then let's go face the firing squad."

When they reached the dining room, Will pulled out her chair for her, then waited while she sat down. To her surprise, he grabbed a wineglass and cleared his throat. "I'd like to propose a toast," he said. "To my Jane, who worked tirelessly to make this a perfect day for everyone. If you appreciate her efforts even half as much as I do, then you'll all make this a perfect day for her, won't you."

Jane felt her cheeks warm at Will's gallant and slightly protective gesture. She glanced over to find him looking down at her, a devilish smile twitching at his lips. There would be no more arguments at the dinner table. He'd see to that. Jane drew a shaky breath and took a sip of her wine. *My Jane.* He'd called her *my Jane.* She'd wanted romantic and he'd managed to provide exactly that.

As she picked at her salad, Jane listened distractedly to the stilted conversation. Lisa and Roy tried to keep things light, while Jane's mother sat mutely at one end of the table and Will's father pouted from the other end. Will seemed happy just to watch Jane eat, his arm draped across the back of her chair, his wine nearly gone. Whenever the conversation moved toward the sensitive subject of the wedding, he deftly turned it back, as if his sole responsibility for the day was to keep Jane happy.

Jane shifted uneasily as her thoughts jumped back to the moments before their guests had arrived. At the time, it had been about desire and release. But now, as she sat in the curve of Will's arm, she wondered if maybe she was missing something. There was no doubt in her mind that Will cared for her. But as she watched him preside over their dinner, taking care to make sure she felt comfortable, Jane realized that maybe his feelings ran deeper than just pure lust. With Will, her physical response to him muddled her mind until she really couldn't see the truths in their relationship. Feelings of simple affection had transformed into desire. But that desire was slowly turning into something much deeper.

Jane glanced over at him again, a shiver coursing through her body. He'd promised they'd continue what they'd started later that evening and Jane found herself looking forward to the moment when they'd be alone again, not so she could break things off with him but so he could fulfill that promise. Then maybe she could look into his eyes and find the truth there.

"Are you all right?" Will whispered.

Jane jumped at the sound of his voice, so close to her ear. "I—I'm fine. I'm just going to get the turkey now." She quickly pushed her chair out and stood, anxious to have something more than memories of seduction to occupy her mind. When she reached the kitchen, Jane opened the freezer and stuck her face inside, breathing in the cold air, letting it clear her head.

Satisfied that she'd regained her composure, Jane turned her attentions to the turkey. But when she moved to the spot where she'd left it, it wasn't there. All that was left on the plate was a puddle of grease. Her heart stopped and her gaze traced a greasy trail along the kitchen floor and into the family room. Jane slowly followed it and when she came around the corner of the sofa, she screamed.

Thurgood lay on the floor, the eighteen-pound turkey resting between his front paws, the carcass nearly gnawed clean. Jane gasped for breath, the shock overwhelming her to the point that she had to sit down. A few seconds later, Will came running into the family room and stopped short when he saw Thurgood.

"Oh, hell," he muttered. Will squatted down and poked at the turkey. "Thurgood, what did you do?" He looked over at Jane. "Can we save it?" He sat back on his heels, waiting for her to weigh in on the situation.

Jane wasn't sure whether to laugh or cry. In the end, exhaustion took control of her emotions and she began to giggle, softly at first and then moving toward hysterical. The entire day had been a disaster. What better way to top it off? Tears flowed from the corners of her eyes and Will slowly got to his feet, an expression of concern etched across his brow.

"Are you all right?" he asked.

Jane waved her hand, a fresh surge of laughter overtaking her. "I'm fine. I'm just great. Well, at least someone's enjoyed the meal. Happy Thanksgiving, Thurgood."

Will took her arm and gently pulled her up, enveloping her in his embrace. "Sweetie, it's all right if you're upset."

"I'm not," Jane said, gasping for breath. "Really."

"Maybe you need to lie down." He pressed his hand to her forehead. "Do you have a fever? Come on, why don't we go upstairs and you can rest? I think all the pressure has gotten to you."

As he led her to the stairs, the rest of the guests came wandering back into the kitchen, curious about the commotion. When Jane's mother saw the turkey on the floor, she went pale. Will's father winced, then scolded the dog. And Jane's father broke out in laughter nearly as hysterical as Jane's.

As Jane passed her father, she pushed up on her toes and gave him a kiss. "Thanks, Daddy," she murmured. Then she grabbed a bottle of wine from the counter and turned to Will. "Why don't you take care of our guests? I'm going to take a nice long bath and drink this wine and try very hard to forget this day."

When Jane reached the relative silence of the second floor, she walked past the bathroom, past her own room, and into Will's. With a soft sigh, she crawled onto his bed and pulled one of his pillows to her chest. She closed her eyes and bent her head, inhaling his scent, her blood warming with thoughts of him.

Right now, she didn't care what was happening downstairs. When the day was all over, it would come down to just the two of them again. Only this time, Jane wasn't going to hold back. She was going to love him, just once, completely and without reservation. And when she remembered this Thanksgiving, she wouldn't remember the sight of Thurgood gobbling up the turkey or the sound of her mother arguing with Will's father. She'd remember Will and sharing something that was more than perfect.

WHEN ALL THE GUESTS had finally departed, Will trudged up the stairs to check on Jane. He peeked into her bedroom, only to find it empty. It had been over an hour since she'd gone upstairs and he'd sent most of the surviving food home with his sister and brother-in-law. But as he and Lisa and Roy had cleaned up, Will's thoughts had focused on Jane.

In truth, he'd been more than a little frightened by her reaction. He could handle tears—and anger. But Jane's laughter was disconcerting considering he had absolutely no idea what was going through her mind. Was she upset with him? Or was she just fed up with the whole situation?

"Jane?" he called.

The bathroom was empty, as well, and since she probably wasn't hanging out in his office, that left only one place—his bedroom. Will walked through his bedroom door and stopped short. She had curled up on his bed and fallen asleep, the half-empty wine bottle sitting on his bedside table. He tiptoed closer and watched her for a long moment, then gave in to the urge to join her. When he was stretched out beside her, Will slipped his arm around her waist and pulled her back against his body.

"Are they gone?" she asked sleepily.

Will rested his chin on her shoulder and nodded. "For a while. I finished cleaning up downstairs. Lisa and Roy just left."

"Thanks," Jane said.

"Are you all right?"

She glanced over her shoulder at him, then twisted around to face him. "It was pretty funny, wasn't it? Was anyone else laughing?"

Will pressed his forehead against hers and gave her a soft kiss. "Your father was. And the kids left laughing. My sister felt badly for you. But your mother managed to hold it together. She didn't cry, though I thought I might need to find some smelling salts."

"And how is Thurgood feeling?"

"Full. Very full. He says you did a great job on the turkey, though. He says it wasn't dry at all and the oyster stuffing is one of his favorites."

Jane smiled, reaching up to smooth her fingertips along his lower lip. "Remind me to thank Thurgood. If it weren't for him, I'd still be down there trying to make everything perfect. I'm not perfect. I never will be, no matter how much my mother wishes I was."

"She loves you, Jane," Will murmured, kissing her fingertips as they caressed his lip. "And she wants the best for you, that's all. She's just like my father. They both want us to be happy."

"I am happy," Jane said. "Here with you, now."

"So am I," he whispered. "Has it been so bad, Janie? I don't know about you, but I think we've been doing pretty well together. Except maybe for today's disaster. But I promised to make it up to you and I will."

"You were going to be my slave for a week, weren't you?"

"Exactly. Now, what would you like me to do? I can massage your feet. Or how about I run you a bath?"

"I have a better idea," Jane said with a lopsided smile. "I want you to take your clothes off."

Will grinned, surprised at the sudden shift in her mood. She must be a lot drunker than she looked. "What?"

"Are you questioning my command?" Jane teased. "I told you to take your clothes off."

Whatever game she'd decided to play, Will was ready to join in. He crawled off the bed and stood beside it, then slowly unbuttoned his shirt and shrugged out of it. When he reached for his belt, she held out her hand to stop him.

"Slowly," Jane said as she sat up. "I want to enjoy this."

Will arched his eyebrow, trying to translate the loopy smile that quirked at her lips. Was this payback for the disastrous day? Was this the wine talking? Or did Jane Singleton finally want him as much as he wanted her? He unhooked his belt and tugged it from the loops, then dangled it in front of her face. "I'm not so sure this falls under the regular duties of a slave. Fetching and carrying, that I can handle. Maybe even a whipping now and then. But I think you might be trying to take advantage of me."

"Now the trousers, Spartacus," she said.

Chuckling, Will kicked off his shoes and socks, then unbuttoned his pants. "Are sure you wouldn't like me to run that bath for you? Or maybe a cold shower?"

"Positive," Jane said.

Will skimmed the trousers over his hips, then kicked out of them, leaving him dressed in only his boxers. "There, are you happy now?"

Jane shook her head and pointed to the boxers. "You're not finished."

He glanced down, noticing his growing erection beneath the silk boxers. Though this had begun as a playful striptease, it was growing increasingly erotic. As she watched him from the bed, he felt both vulnerable and powerful. Will knew that if he wanted to, he could reach out and touch her and she'd surrender. But for now, she held the control and he was happy to let her keep it.

His gaze fixed on Jane's face, Will stripped off the last bit of clothing, then waited, his heart slamming in his chest. "Better?"

"Mmm," she said, crawling to her knees. "Much better." Jane slipped off the bed and slowly circled him, allowing her fingers to drift gently across his skin. The fleeting caress only served to excite him more and Will reached out to grab her, but she danced away.

"Ah, ah, ah," she warned. "I don't think you're supposed to touch me."

He growled, the sound rumbling low in his throat. "This is a dangerous game you're playing."

"Is it?"

Will watched as Jane slowly unbuttoned her blouse, revealing the soft shoulders that he'd kissed just that morning. His fingers clenched instinctively, but he knew he couldn't touch her. Drawing a deep breath, he tried to focus his thoughts elsewhere, afraid that he'd come just watching her undress.

He thought he knew Jane, but every day, she seemed to reveal something more to him, another layer of her intriguing personality. How could a woman be so incredibly sweet one moment and then tantalizingly seductive the next? And how could she be both friend and lover at the same time?

The last item of clothing fell to the floor and Jane stood in front of him, still smiling. With deliberate ease, she let her fingers drift from his collarbone, down his chest to his belly, and then lower. She closed her hand around his hard shaft and gently stroked him, her touch featherlight. He ached to touch her, but instead, focused his mind on the sensations that coursed through his body.

When he didn't think he could take any more, when his breath came in short gasps, she stopped. But then a moment later, she took him into her mouth and he felt a shock wave course through his body. He groaned, then murmured her name as he raked his fingers through her soft hair. As he felt himself nearing the edge of his control, Jane took him deeper. "Sweetheart, stop," he pleaded, his voice raw with desire.

She slowly stood, then took his hand and drew him to the bed. Pressing her palms against his shoulders, she pushed him down until he sat on the edge of the mattress. His eyes fixed on hers, Will slipped his arm around her waist. He settled her on his lap, her legs pressed against his hips.

For a long time, they did nothing but kiss and touch, exploring each other's bodies with lips and fingertips.

And when she finally unrolled the condom over his rigid shaft and he slipped inside of her, Will was certain of one thing. He loved Jane—and he never wanted to let her go.

As she moved above him, Will watched her, the myriad of expressions that colored her face, the tiny sounds that slipped from her throat. She belonged to him, body and soul. And when he reached between them and touched her, Will brought her to the edge, losing himself in her heat and damp.

They came together in an explosion of shattering need, her body convulsing around his as he drove into her one last time. Will held her close, his arms wrapped around her waist, his face nestled between her breasts. "I love you, Jane," he murmured against her skin. "I do. I love you."

He pulled her down on the bed, drawing her body against his and tucking her chin into the curve of his neck. And then he waited, praying that she'd return the sentiment and that her feelings would match his. But silence descended around them. She wasn't asleep. Her breathing hadn't slowed, nor had her body relaxed. In the end, Will understood the truth—that no matter how much he wanted her, she couldn't love him back.

Something—or someone—still stood in the way.

JANE WOKE UP LONG BEFORE DAWN, lying in Will's arms and listening to him breathe in and out while she contemplated the decision she had to make. He loved her. He'd said the words, but Jane couldn't let herself believe they were true.

How many times had he professed his love for one girl or another, certain that she was the one? Will McCaffrey fell in love as quickly as he fell out of it. And if she allowed herself to believe his words, then she'd be lost for good, caught in a fantasy that might never become reality. She'd spent nearly a third of her life believing that Will was the only man who could ever make her happy. And now that he was so close she could reach out and touch him, she'd suddenly stopped believing.

Her temples throbbed from the wine she'd drunk the night before and tears pressed at the corners of her eyes. But she refused to surrender to her emotions. She couldn't stay any longer, not without risking everything. Just the thought of seeing him every day, of being tempted to experience this passion just one last time, was too much to bear.

She reached out and smoothed her fingers over his beard-roughened cheek. He stirred slightly and she drew away, her gaze still fixed on his face. "I love you, too. I always have and I probably always will."

Jane held her breath as she slipped out of bed. To her relief, he continued to sleep and she stood over him and watched, taking in every last detail of his face and his hands, the body that had made her shudder with desire. She'd always wanted just one perfect night with Will and now, she'd experienced so much more. It was time to leave, to put her fantasies in the past and get on with real life.

Drawing a shaky breath, Jane turned away from the bed and walked to her room, marshalling her resolve with every step. She slowly dressed as she packed an overnight bag, wondering at how familiar her surroundings had become. This had been her home and she'd felt safe here. For a short time, she'd had everything she'd ever dreamed of.

Jane bit her lower lip to stave off more tears. She still had her friends and her family. Maybe she'd stay with Lisa and Roy or maybe she'd go home and break the bad news to her mother. Either way, she'd have to make some plans for her future—a fresh start maybe in a new city. Time hadn't diminished her feelings for Will—perhaps distance would.

"Jane?"

She spun around, the sound of Will's voice startling her in the quiet of the house. He was dressed in just his boxers, riding low on his hips, his chest bare.

"You weren't there when I woke up," he murmured, rubbing his eyes sleepily. His gaze came to rest on the clothes she clutched, then moved to the open bag on the bed. "What are you doing?"

"I—I'm packing," Jane said, her voice trembling slightly. "I have to go."

Will took a step into the room. He clenched his hands at his sides, as if he wanted to make sure he couldn't touch her. "Vacation?" he asked. He held up his hand to stop her reply. "Right. Never mind. I guess I should have known."

"What do you mean?"

He laughed harshly, then shook his head. "You've been halfway out the door ever since you moved in here. It seems that every time we take a step toward each other, you take two steps back to the door. It's like this little dance we do."

"I—I just can't live here anymore. It's all too confusing. I don't know who I am or what I feel. I don't know if I'm staying because I want to stay or because I've been forced to."

"I never forced you, Jane."

"You didn't give me any choice. That's the same thing."

"You could have said no," he murmured.

"Why? So you would take me to court? When I moved in here, I had nothing left. My business was failing, I couldn't pay the rent on my apartment, my car was broken and I didn't have the money to fix it. This just seemed like a convenient place to wait it out until business picked up in the spring."

He pressed his lips into a tight line and nodded. "So you used me?"

"No more than you used me. Don't forget why you came looking for me, Will. You needed a wife so your father would give you the company."

"So maybe our motives weren't the best. But things have changed, Jane. Can't you see that?"

"No. We started out wrong and everything that's happened since then is wrong."

"Jane, come on," he said, an angry edge in his voice. "I felt you there with me last night. That wasn't an act. That's who you are, that woman who seduced me, who made me ache to touch her. What the hell changed between last night and this morning?"

"Nothing. And everything."

"Do you think you could be more specific?"

"You said you loved me," she shouted, her fists

clenched, her tone accusatory, as if his words had been more an insult than an endearment.

"Considering what we were doing, wasn't that a good thing?"

"How many women have you said that to? How many women have you professed your love to, only to dump them a few weeks later? Those words may work on other women, but I know you too well, Will."

"None," he said.

"None? What do you mean, none?"

"I've never said those words to another woman, Jane. You're the first. Hell, you might just be the last."

"Don't lie to me! I had to sit there and listen to you discuss every one of them. Each of them had been perfect until something changed your mind. Her hair was too curly, her feet too big. She dressed too conservatively, she didn't dress conservatively enough. It was always something with you. What's it going to be with me?"

"I'll admit, there have been a lot of women in my life," Will said. "I can't change the past. But I can control the future. And I do love you."

She stiffened her spine, refusing to accept his declaration. "I don't believe you. Maybe you think you love me now, but it won't last."

Will crossed the room in three long steps and grabbed her arms. "Don't tell me what I feel! And don't tell me how long it's going to last! Damn it, Jane, what do you want from me?"

"I—I want more. I want—" She groaned and turned away from him. "I don't know what I want. But I don't want this. I don't want to feel forced to live here because I can't afford a lawyer. I don't want to feel angry that the only reason you want to marry me is because of your father. I just...want more."

Will sat down on the edge of the bed and rubbed his eyes. "You want him, don't you? You'd rather live in some fantasy world with a guy you can never have, than live a real life with me."

"You don't know anything about him," she muttered, turning back to her packing. She wasn't sure what to say to Will. She fought the urge to tell him the truth, that he was the boy she'd loved all those years ago, the one she'd written about in her journals. But maybe it was best to keep her little secret, convincing him he was right, that she did love someone else. "I just want more from a relationship than you can give me. I want to know I'll never be hurt or disappointed. I promised to stay for three months, and I haven't even managed a month. But I know how I feel, Will, and more time together isn't going to change my mind."

Will nodded, his anger gone, replaced by resignation. "I understand. Hey, I was crazy to think this was going to work. You have your life, I have mine. And we signed that contract too long ago." He rubbed the back of his neck and winced. "No hard feelings?"

"None," Jane murmured, stunned by his sudden shift in mood. Her heart ached as she realized that she'd seen it before. It was what he'd always done when he was finished with a relationship, the cool withdrawal of his affections, the indifferent facade.

"Where are you going to go?"

Jane shrugged. "I'm not sure. Lisa offered her sofa. Or I could go home to my parents. I'll be all right."

He slowly stood, then reached out to touch her. But at the last minute, he drew his hand away. "If there's anything you need, Janie, I want you to call me. After all this, I still want us to be friends."

"Right back where we started." Jane pushed up on her toes and kissed his cheek. "Goodbye, Will."

With that, she grabbed her bag and walked out of the room, not bothering to pack the rest of her things. As she hurried down the stairs, every instinct told her to turn around, to run back to Will and accept what he was offering, to stay with the man she loved, even if it was only for a short time.

But in the end, she walked out. After all, she'd already risked too much and she wasn't willing to risk the ultimate price—her heart.

8

THE JOB SITE WAS CRAWLING with activity when Will arrived. Excavation had begun and heavy machinery moved in and out of the gates, the dump trucks rumbling as they passed, the crew shouting instructions. They had been desperate to break ground on the project before the New Year since McCaffrey Commercial Properties was already three months behind schedule. And Will had been lucky that the project had consumed so much time. It kept his mind off Jane.

Will leaned back against the door of his car, his gaze fixed unseeingly on a crane that hung above the site. It had been more than a month since she'd walked out and he still hadn't come to grips with what had happened between them. He'd picked up the phone countless times to call her, but each attempt had been mired in self-doubt and aborted before dialing.

Hell, he knew how she felt. No matter how hard he pushed, Jane wasn't going to love him. "Never did, never will," Will murmured. No, Jane was in love with a man she couldn't have. The lure of an unattainable man was stronger than the possibility of a future with a guy standing right in front of her. Will pulled his overcoat more tightly around him, warding off the frigid breeze. "And now I know exactly how that feels," he murmured.

The diagnosis was easy. But the cure for this little disease called Jane Singleton was much harder to find. He'd thought about losing himself in another woman, about pulling out the little black book and getting back to what he'd always done best. But the prospect seemed oddly unappealing.

Will chuckled softly. "She ruined me," he murmured. God, he used to think guys were such saps when they wallowed in the aftermath of a relationship gone bad. And now, that's exactly what he was doing—wallowing.

"I thought I'd find you here."

Will twisted around to see his father approach, holding a hard hat in his hand. He gave the hat to Will and then rapped his knuckles on his own hat. "Safety first," he joked.

"I told you I'd stop by and talk to the engineers. You didn't have to come all the way out here."

"Yes, I did," Jim McCaffrey said, hitching his arm up on the roof of the car. "I needed to talk to you—outside the office."

"What is it now?" Will asked. "'Cause I really don't want to get into another one of our father-son fights. I'm just not up for it today."

"Then I think you're going to need earplugs along with that hard hat, because you're not going to like what I have to say." Jim McCaffrey paused, staring down at the toes of his shoes while he contemplated his next words. "So I'm just going to come right out and say it. I don't think it's a good idea for you to marry that Singleton girl. Her father is nice enough, but after meeting her mother, I have to say, I can't see spending another holiday with her. And this whole thing about Christmas. If you two are going to be married, then her mother can't dictate where Jane spends the holidays. Hell, Will, you and Jane weren't even together on Christmas Eve."

Will chuckled at the irony. "Well, you won't have to worry about that, Dad. Because I'm not going to marry Jane Singleton. She dumped me the day after Thanksgiving and I haven't seen her since."

"She dumped you? Over a month ago? And you haven't said anything?"

"Yes, yes, and…yes. I guess I didn't want to hear the same old speech about how I'm ruining my life."

Jim frowned. "Well, I'm sorry. But I think you're going to consider that a lucky break. They say you can tell a lot about how a woman is going to be in twenty years by looking at her mother. And I'd hate to think you'd be putting up with *that* when you're my age, all that weeping and carrying on. Now, your grandmother, she was the sweetest woman in the world. Practical and levelheaded. When I met her, I knew your mother would be the same. Jane Singleton, on the other hand, will turn into her mother in her old age, mark my words."

Will straightened and turned on his father, his rage bubbling over. "Where do you get off talking about Jane that way? You don't even know her. She's sweet and kind and sensitive. And maybe she is a bit of a perfectionist and a little too emotional and a complete romantic. But she was the best thing that ever happened to me."

"You may think so, but I—"

"I don't give a crap what you think. This is *my* life we're talking about and I make the decisions in my personal life. I may not be able to control the decisions you make regarding my professional life, but I sure as hell control the ones I make when it comes to Jane. So just butt out, Dad."

"I can't do that," he said.

"What? Now you want final approval on the bride I pick? Hell, why don't I just leave it all up to you? You can go out and find me a wife. I'll just show up for the wedding and live miserably-ever-after."

Jim shook his head. "I want you to forget what I said, Will. I was wrong."

"About what?"

"About everything. You need to find a bride in your own good time, without my interference. And I need to realize that your personal life has nothing at all to do with your professional competence. I talked to Ronald this morning and told him I was going to name you CEO in April. He understood and assured me that you have his full backing."

Will stared at his father, his mouth agape, astonished by the sudden turn of events. "That's it? No strings, no demands?"

"That's it. We'll start to work on the transition to-morrow. I want you to handle pitching the Denver project. That one will be all yours. And you need to meet with our financial backers before the end of the week. They've been a little skittish since they heard I wanted to retire."

Will held up his hand. "Hold on. I'm not sure I want to accept the job."

"What?"

"I've been thinking about striking out on my own."

"Why would you want to do that?" Jim asked. "I'm giving you everything I've spent my life building." He clapped Will on the shoulder. "Take it and run before I change my mind. And get on with your life. The past is the past."

Will watched as his father strode through the gates and onto the job site. He still couldn't believe what he'd heard. Yesterday, Will had been seriously contemplating quitting, just picking up his pencils and taking them somewhere new. But now, everything he'd wanted was right here, right in front him.

"Not everything," Will murmured. He got the job, but he didn't get the girl.

Still, he was right back where he had started a few months ago. If he just put his time with Jane out of his mind, maybe his life could get back to normal. He'd start dating again, open himself to the possibilities of a long-term relationship. And then someday, he'd meet a woman who would make him forget all about Jane Singleton.

He wasn't going to spend the rest of his life lugging this torch around. Like Jane, he was moving on.

"ARE YOU SURE WE SHOULD BE here?" Lisa whispered.

"I have to pick up the rest of my things," Jane said,

pushing the key into the lock. "You want me to do that while he's here?"

"Why not just leave them? What's so important that you can't do without?"

"My plants," Jane said. "I want my plants back."

"Honey, it's been more than a month since you left. Don't you think they might be dead?"

Jane froze, then turned to Lisa. "You actually think he'd be mean enough to let them die?"

Lisa grabbed Jane by the shoulders and gave her a little shake. "He's a guy, and you dumped him. I think the last thing he's going to do is water your plants."

"Well, I'm not going to leave without them, dead or not. I've had some of those plants almost as long as I've had you as a friend. I'd never think of abandoning you." She drew a deep breath. "Now, I have to shut off the security system. Hopefully, he hasn't changed the code."

"And if he has?"

"Then run," Jane replied. She opened the front door and quickly reached for the keypad. She punched in the number Will had given her the night she moved in and to her relief, the system was disarmed. "All right, we're in."

"Why does this feel like breaking and entering?" Lisa asked, shuffling in behind Jane.

"We're not doing anything illegal. I have a key. I know the security code. And I have property here. Legally, I don't think the police would be able to arrest us."

"And this from a woman who couldn't get out of a

six-year-old handwritten marriage contract. I'm not so sure I trust your legal expertise."

Jane reached back and grabbed Lisa's hand, then pulled her toward the stairs. "Thurgood should be around here somewhere. He's not much of a guard dog. But usually he comes to the door when he hears someone outside."

"Why are we whispering and tiptoeing if there's no one here?" Lisa asked.

"I don't know." With a soft curse, Jane straightened and quickly climbed the stairs. "Let's just get my plants and leave."

When they reached her bedroom door, Jane stopped short. A soft thumping noise caught her attention. "What's that?" She spun around to see Thurgood standing in the doorway of Will's room, his tail banging up against the doorjamb. He trotted up to her and nuzzled her hand and Jane bent down and scratched his ears. "Good doggy."

"Stop playing with the dog," Lisa hissed as she opened the door to Jane's bedroom. "Oh, my God."

Jane quickly stood. "What?" She pushed past Lisa and stepped inside. "Oh, my." Her plants were scattered around the room, exactly as she had left them. "They're alive." She hurried over to Anya and stuck her finger into the soil. "He's been watering them. They look good." Jane fought back a surge of emotion. "He took care of my plants."

Lisa pulled a wad of plastic grocery bags out of her jacket pocket and handed them to Jane. "Here. I'll bundle them up. You get your clothes and your stuff from the bathroom."

"I can't believe he watered my plants. Do you think he hoped I'd come back?"

"I don't know what he was thinking," Lisa said. She crossed the room to Jane, turned her around and pushed her toward the door. "Just move it. I don't want to stay here any longer than we have to."

Jane stumbled out of the bedroom and headed down the hall to the bathroom. She caught sight of her reflection in the mirror and her mind flashed back to the memory of Will seducing her in this very spot. Jane ran her hands over the counter and let the memories flood back. A blush warmed her cheeks and she took a ragged breath then turned back to the door. There wasn't anything in the bathroom she was attached to anyway.

But as she rushed out into the hall, she ran face first into a naked chest. A scream slipped from her throat and Jane jumped back, her heart grinding to a stop as her gaze took in Will.

"Jane?"

Her eyes slowly rose, from his bare feet to his long legs to the silk boxers and then onto his chest, which was still a little red from where she'd bumped into him. "Will," she murmured, risking a glance higher as she rubbed her nose. "What are you doing here?"

A smile teased at his lips. "I live here. What are *you* doing here?"

"I—I just came to pick up a few of my things. I didn't expect you'd be here. It's the middle of the day."

"What the heck is going—"

They both turned to watch Lisa emerge from the bedroom. Her eyes went wide as she took in the scene, her gaze darting back and forth between Jane's stunned expression and Will's half-naked body. "Hi, Will."

He nodded in her direction. "Hi, Lisa."

"I—I want you to know this wasn't my idea. In fact, I told Jane I thought we might be breaking the law. So if you're going to call the cops, be sure to tell them that I was an unwitting accomplice."

He chuckled as he rubbed his bare chest. "I'll do that."

"We didn't realize you'd be home," Jane explained, "or we never would have come in."

"I had a late night last night. And I have a business trip scheduled for this afternoon. I'm flying to Denver to pitch a project. In fact, I'm probably going to be spending a lot of time out there if we get the job." Will paused as if waiting for Jane to comment. "I do have good news. My father named me CEO. I take over officially in April or May."

"Wow," Jane said. "That's great."

"Yeah, great," Lisa added. "You must be so happy. But why would you want to move from Chicago? I mean, wouldn't you miss..." They both glanced over at Lisa and she immediately took her cue. "I'll just finish up in the bedroom."

"So, you got everything you wanted," Jane murmured, nervously shifting her gaze to her hands.

He took a step closer and leaned against the wall. "Nearly everything," he replied.

"Well, I'm thinking of moving, too," she said softly.

"You are?"

He dipped his head to try to catch her eyes and Jane reluctantly looked up at him. The moment she met his gaze, her heart skipped a beat and then another. He was so close. If she wanted, she could just lean forward a bit, tip her head up and part her lips and he'd— "It's difficult to make a seasonal business like ours work in this climate. So if I want to do what I do best, I'm going to have to go someplace warm. Like Florida or California. Although, it's a whole new world there. There would be new plants to learn about and new insects and diseases and..." She let her voice trail off as soon as she realized she'd begun babbling.

"Then we're both moving on," Will said. "That's good."

She nodded. "Very good."

"So where are you staying?"

"Why?"

"I just thought I should know in case you leave anything behind. I can send it over."

"At Lisa and Roy's place in Wicker Park." He nodded and a long silence grew between them. Jane scrambled for another topic of conversation but her heart was pounding so hard she couldn't think. All she could really do is wait and wonder if he felt as nervous as she did. She swallowed hard. "Well, I should get going."

"Me, too." He reached out and took her hand, lacing his fingers through hers. "It was nice to see you again, Jane. Nice to have you back in the house, if only for a little while."

Jane fought the urge to pull him closer, to step into an embrace that she hoped would be there if she did.

But nothing in his manner made her believe that he'd welcome such a move. Reluctantly she let go of his hand and walked back to the bedroom. Before she stepped inside, she glanced back, but Will had already disappeared down the stairs.

"Well," Lisa whispered, "how did it go?"

"Just grab the plants and let's get out of here." Her voice wavered slightly and Jane covered with a soft cough. "He said he'd send me the rest of my things."

She grabbed three of the plastic bags and headed for the stairs. The trip from there to the street in front of Will's house was all a blur of tightly checked emotion. She paced back and forth on the sidewalk, waiting for Lisa to emerge, impatient to put herself as far away from Will McCaffrey as possible. When Lisa finally stepped out of the door, Jane started toward the truck.

"Wait up," Lisa called, running after her.

Jane bit back a curse as she stumbled slightly. "Did you see that?"

"Yeah," Lisa said. "He's got an incredible body. Jeez, Jane, how did you ever keep your hands off that night after night?"

"I'm not talking about his body! I'm talking about his…demeanor. So cool, so distant. He had a late night last night. What do you think that means?"

"He stayed out past his usual bedtime?"

"He was with a woman! Couldn't you tell? He looked…satisfied."

"He looked groggy, like he'd just gotten out of bed."

"My point exactly." Jane shook her head, trying to banish the memory of him from her head. "It's obvious he's moved on. He's forgotten everything we shared and he's moved on."

"You don't know that. Maybe he was working late or maybe he just got in from out of town. Maybe he stayed up and watched a movie."

"Why are you defending him?" Jane said, turning on her friend.

Lisa held up her hands in mock surrender. "I'm not. I'm just saying you shouldn't be so quick to jump to conclusions. I was there. I heard what he said. I also saw the way he looked at you."

"And how was that?"

"As if he couldn't look away," Lisa murmured. "The whole time I watched you two talking, he never once took his eyes off you, Jane. He looked like—"

"He was angry?"

"No, he looked like a man in love."

The breath caught in her throat and Jane started off down the sidewalk again. "Don't say that. I'm not going to let myself get caught up in that fantasy all over again. I am over him. Whatever I felt is gone. I'm moving on with my life and he's moving on with his, end of story, period."

"And you are such a liar," Lisa shouted for everyone to hear. "By the way, you missed the car. It's right here."

Jane stopped short, then turned and strode back to Lisa's car. "I don't want to hear any more about this, understand?" From this moment on, she was going to stop thinking and dreaming and fantasizing about Will McCaffrey. It was a promise she'd make to herself and a promise she intended to keep!

"ARE YOU GOING TO SPEND the rest of your life lying on that sofa?"

Jane looked up at Lisa and sighed. "Nope. Just the next month or two, until business picks up."

She'd been living at Roy and Lisa's for two months now, sharing the cramped quarters of the tiny apartment and sleeping on their lumpy sofa. On weekends, Jane usually went to her parents', hoping to give Lisa and her husband some precious time alone. But two nights with her mother was all she could bear and she always ended up back on Lisa's sofa on Monday night.

"*If* business picks up." Lisa flopped down on a well-worn easy chair and kicked her feet up on the coffee table. "What are we going to do about business, Jane? We have to talk about this."

Jane slowly sat up and reached for the remote, switching off her videotape of *Wait Until Dark* and turning her attention to her business partner and best friend. "I don't know. I want to believe we can make this work, but I'm starting to think that a business our size just can't survive without winter work."

"I suppose we could always fold sweaters at the Gap," Lisa offered. She paused. "Or I could go work for Roy's company."

"What?"

"I've been meaning to tell you. Their office manager just quit and Roy asked if I'd come to work with him. The business is really expanding and the pay would be better than what I'm making now—which is basically nothing." Lisa bit her bottom lip and blinked back tears. "If you don't want me to, I won't, Jane. Windy

City Gardens was our dream and I don't want to let it go until you do."

"No," Jane said, reaching out to take her friend's hand. "It's time. Besides, I've been thinking about getting a fresh start. Maybe moving down south, finding a place where gardens grow twelve months of the year."

"You'd move?" Lisa asked.

"There's not much keeping me here."

"What about Will?"

"What about him?"

"You still love him. I think you've always loved him."

"That doesn't mean I have to continue loving him," Jane said. "It's time for me to smarten up and move on with my life. There are a lot of fish in the sea. I just have to swim out and find them. Besides, he's the one who gave me the idea. He said he'd be spending more time out of state and I told him I was thinking of moving, even though that was a lie at the time. But it's not a bad idea."

Lisa glanced at her watch, then looked over at the clock on the VCR.

"Are you late for something?" Jane asked.

"No," she said. "I just—"

The doorbell rang, interrupting her reply and Lisa scrambled out of the chair and crossed the room. But before she opened the door, she turned back to Jane. "I think you might want to run a comb through your hair. And brush those cookie crumbs off your pajamas."

"Why?"

"Because Will is here."

"What?" Jane gasped.

"Don't get angry. He called the other day and said

he had something of yours he wanted to return, so I told him he could drop by. You have to talk to him, Jane. If only to bring closure to all these feelings you've had for him. How can you even think about moving on until you do?" She let her gaze fix on Jane's. "Unless, of course, you don't want to move on."

The doorbell sounded again and Jane quickly got to her feet. "Don't let him in," she warned.

"I personally think he's in love with you," Lisa said. "And I know you're in love with him. But the both of you are just too stubborn to admit it."

"You know Will as well as I do. He's not capable of love. At least not in the long term."

"How do you know that? You lived with him for less than a month and nothing in his behavior proved that. Did he run around with other women? Did he stay out all night with his buddies? Did he ever once make you feel as if you couldn't trust him?"

"No, but that doesn't mean—"

"What? What doesn't it mean? Because from where I stand, I see a man who has grown up a lot in the past six years. A man who might just be ready to make that commitment if you'd just give him the chance. Now, I suggest you go into the bathroom and comb your hair, maybe put on a little lipstick while I let him in."

Jane let out a yelp and grabbed a sweater and jeans from her suitcase in the corner of the room. A few seconds later, she slammed the bathroom door behind her and quickly stripped out of her flannel pajamas. There wasn't time for a shower so she splashed water on her face and raked her fingers through her tousled hair.

Her heart slammed in her chest and she felt a bit

light-headed, but she forced herself to maintain her cool. It had been nearly a month since she'd last seen Will but that hadn't stopped her from thinking about him. She'd hoped he might call, but there had been no contact, nothing to indicate what he was doing...and who he might be doing it with.

She tugged on her sweater and jeans, then grabbed a bottle of perfume and dabbed a bit on her neck and wrists. Then she sat down on the edge of the tub and tried to regain her composure. It wasn't as if this was a date or anything. He'd just stopped by to drop something off. "So then why does it feel like a date?" she muttered.

A soft knock sounded on the bathroom door and a moment later, Lisa slipped inside. "Are you going to stay in here all night?"

"How does he look?" Jane asked. "I mean, does he look like he's spoiling for a fight? Or does he look happy?"

"He's gorgeous," Lisa said. "If I wasn't married, I'd think about locking you in here so I could steal him for myself. And he looks like he's anxious to see you."

"Anxiously nervous or anxiously optimistic."

Lisa groaned, then grabbed Jane's hand and pulled her to the door. "Out," she said. "Go talk to him. And try to be nice." Lisa shoved her through the door, then slammed it behind her so she couldn't come back in.

Drawing a deep breath, Jane walked into the living room. He was standing near the sofa, his back to her. "Hi," she said.

Will turned and smiled. "Hi, Jane."

Hesitantly she crossed the room and circled the sofa.

They stood together in uneasy silence, before they both sat down.

"How have you been?" Jane asked.

He reached out and took her hand, as if he suddenly needed to touch her. "I've been good. Busy with work."

"Me, too. Very busy."

He paused and then drew a deep breath. "I've missed you, Jane. I guess I got used to having you around the house."

"All those great home-cooked meals and my outstanding decorating taste?"

"Right," Will said. "All that. And a lot of other stuff, too. And Thurgood misses you, too." He let go of her hand and grabbed a bag he'd set on the coffee table. "Here, I brought you this. It's your *Breakfast at Tiffany's* tape. You left it in the VCR."

Jane took it from his hand. "Thanks. I haven't been in the mood to watch this, so I hadn't missed it."

"I got you something else," Will said. "Kind of a belated Christmas gift. Although, it's almost Valentine's Day, so I suppose it could be for that holiday, too."

"You didn't need to buy me a gift," Jane said. "I didn't get you anything."

He grabbed the bag and handed it to her. "I didn't have time to wrap it. Actually I didn't have any paper to wrap it in and I'm not even sure I could wrap it if I—" He grinned and shook his head. "Well, just open it."

Jane peeked inside and pulled out a small box, a DVD of *Breakfast at Tiffany's*. She found *Roman Holiday* and *Sabrina* in the bag as well.

"I remembered how much you like Audrey Hepburn. I also got you a DVD player. It's in the car. You should really have the latest in technology. And there's a lot of interesting extra features on the DVDs that the videos don't have."

Jane leaned over and kissed Will on the cheek. "Thank you. Audrey Hepburn is my favorite."

"I remember," he said.

He grabbed her hand again and drew it up to his mouth to kiss her fingertips. Moment by moment, touch by touch, they were moving closer to something, but Jane wasn't sure what it was. "So, how have you been?" he asked.

"Good," she repeated. "Busy with work. I've been looking for a new apartment. I think Lisa and Roy are getting a little tired of me taking up room on their sofa."

His expression registered surprise. "I thought you were going to move."

"That's still up in the air yet. I haven't made a decision one way or the other."

"I could help you with that," Will offered. "Finding an apartment. We work with a few property management companies. Whenever you're ready just…"

"Call you," Jane finished. "I will."

He glanced around nervously. "I should probably go. I just wanted to drop that video by and, you know, check in, see how you were."

"Well, I'm fine," Jane said.

He got up and started toward the door, then changed his mind and moved back to the sofa, pulling her up to stand in front of him. "Jane, I know you're

still in love with him. And I can understand how difficult it is for you to forget him. Hell, I don't think I'm
going to be forgetting you anytime soon." He rubbed
his right biceps. "I think I might have to start weight
training so I can carry that torch around for the rest of
my life."

"Will, I—"

He sat back down, drawing her with him, then
pressed his finger to her lips. "I don't need any expla-
nations, Jane, or any promises right now. I just want to
tell you that your happiness is the most important
thing to me in the world. And if you can't be happy
with me, then I want you to be happy with this other
guy." Will gently wove her fingers through his. "So, is
he married? Is that why you can't be together?"

Jane shook her head. Every ounce of common sense
told her that she should tell Will the entire story about
the "other man." But it was embarrassing to admit
she'd been madly in love with Will from the moment
she'd first met him. And that she'd carried that love
around with her for six years. "He's not."

"That's good," Will said.

"Why?"

"Because you need to go to him. If you don't know
where he is, then we're going to track him down and
you're going to tell him how you feel. And he can tell
you how he feels. And once you both do that, then you
can move on with your life."

"What if he feels the same way about me as I do
about him?" Jane asked.

Will shrugged. "I guess I'll have to deal with that.
But I'm hoping he doesn't and you'll realize what we

have together is better than anything you'll ever have with him."

"I know where he is," Jane said. "I suppose I could go talk to him."

"That's good." Will slowly drew back and looked down into her eyes. He was so close, she could feel his breath on her lips, just a heartbeat away from kissing her. She waited, praying that he'd capture her mouth with his and end this sweet torment. And when he let go of her hands and stood, Jane tried to hide her disappointment.

Forcing a smile, she walked to the door with him. "Thanks for stopping by."

"I'm just going to go down and get your DVD player."

"No," Jane said, determined that this wouldn't be the last time they saw each other. "You can bring it up the next time you come."

A slow grin curled the corners of his mouth. "All right then. Till next time." He gave her hand a squeeze, then slipped out into the hallway. Jane closed the door behind him and leaned back against it.

"Is he gone?"

Jane looked up as Lisa hurried back into the room. "He's gone."

"So how did it go?" Lisa asked. "Did you work things out?"

"No, not really. But at least we're still friends. And I guess, if I want more, then I'm going to have to decide between Will and the other man in my life," she said, bemused.

"What other man?"

"There is no other man," Jane said, flopping back down on the sofa.

Lisa tipped her head to the side and frowned. "Did I miss something?"

"Will thinks I'm in love with someone else, that I've been carrying a torch for this guy since college. Somehow, my mother found my journals and read them and then she told Will I was in love with a boy from college with the initials P.C."

"But you were in love with Will in college," Lisa said.

"Right. P.C. Prince Charming. That's what I used to call him in my journals."

"So Will thinks you were in love with—"

"Will. Only he doesn't know it's Will—or himself. And now he wants me to find this guy—Will—and tell him how I feel. Because I can't move forward with Will until I put—Will behind me."

"So which Will was here tonight?"

"They're one and the same."

"And which one do you love?" Lisa asked.

"I love them both—the Will I used to know and the Will I know now." Jane felt tears flood her eyes, but this time, she didn't try to stop them. "I do love him. I guess I really didn't realize that until I saw him tonight."

"So, do I get to be a bridesmaid or what?" Lisa asked. "And don't tell me you have to ask your mother."

Jane smiled through her tears. "If I marry Will, I think maybe Las Vegas would be a good option."

Lisa covered her mouth with her hand, feigning an

expression of pure horror. "Bite your tongue! If you get married in Vegas your mother will never forgive you, and neither will I."

A giggle slipped from Jane's lips and a moment later, she and Lisa had dissolved into laughter. Everything was going to be all right. For the first time since the whole contract mess had started, Jane believed that she and Will might actually have a chance together. Now, she just had to figure out a way to make that happen.

9

WILL PACED BACK AND FORTH across the width of his office, his attention fixed on his desk calendar. He'd been counting down the days since he'd last seen Jane, ticking them off one by one until he flipped the calendar over to February 4. "Not too early, not too late," he murmured. At least according to all the etiquette research he'd done on the Internet.

Asking a woman for a date had never been so complicated, but this was one invitation Will didn't want to mess up. Especially since it involved a major holiday. The recommended lead time was at least a week. Will figured that if Jane had any other offers, they'd come in about that time. So he'd decided on ten days. "Not too early, not too late."

He stopped pacing and looked over at the phone. Why not call her and get it over with? He had Lisa's number and Jane was probably home from work by now. Unless...

Will cursed softly. What if she'd stopped for drinks with Torch Boy? He'd thought about the guy so many times over the past few weeks that Will had decided to give him a name. Torch Boy. The recipient of Jane's undying devotion, the man she just couldn't stop loving. Only Jane's happiness had been on his mind when Will had suggested she call him. But when she'd agreed to his proposal, he'd been left to regret his suggestion, kicking himself in the ass at the top of every waking hour.

There was one way to find out where he stood, Will mused. He had to pick up the phone and call her. "Do it," he murmured, psyching himself up. But when he reached for the phone, he froze. This wasn't just any date. This was probably the most important date of his life, so he'd better make sure he didn't sound like an idiot in the asking.

Will sat down at his desk and pulled out a piece of paper, then quickly scribbled a few notes. He'd ask her how she was, he'd mention that he still had her DVD player in the trunk of his car, he'd say he'd been thinking about her a lot lately—and then he'd ask. "So, Jane, do you have any plans for Valentine's Day?" Will murmured.

Hell, he had to be able to come up with something a little more romantic than that! "Think," he muttered. Suddenly every ounce of his charm and ease with women had drained out of his body. And if he waited for it to come back, then he might miss his window of opportunity.

Will grabbed the phone, punched in Lisa's number and waited as it rang on the other end.

"Hello?"

He recognized Roy's voice immediately and breathed a silent sigh of relief. "Hey, Roy, it's Will McCaffrey."

"Will! How are you?"

"Good. I was wondering if Jane was around."

"She is," Roy said. "She's helping Lisa with dinner. Would you like to talk to her?"

Will drew in a deep breath. "Yeah, I would." He heard Roy call Jane's name and a few seconds later, the muffled sound of a hand over the receiver. Finally, when Jane came on the line, Will's heart jumped up into his throat.

"Hello?" she said.

"Hi, Jane." Will picked up his pen and furiously began to doodle on the legal pad in front of him. He forgot his notes, forgot everything he wanted to say and scrambled for a decent opening line. "How are you?"

"I'm fine, Will. How are you?"

He ignored the question, choosing to get right to the point. "Do you have any plans for Valentine's Day?"

Another silence from her end and Will counted off the seconds. It felt like a lifetime, but in truth, he'd just reached three when she spoke again. "No, I don't."

"Would you like to go out?"

"With you?"

"Yes, with me. I thought we could have dinner, maybe find a place to go dancing. You do dance, don't you?"

"I guess so."

He groaned inwardly. This was not going well at all. Jane sounded about as enthused as a woman facing a root canal. "So?"

"All right. I think that would be fun. What time?"

"I'll pick you up at Lisa and Roy's at seven. February 14. Valentine's Day. It's a Saturday night. Is that all right?"

She giggled softly. "That's great. I'll look forward to it. Bye, Will."

"Bye," he said. He quickly slammed the phone down, then leaned forward to rest his forehead on the cool surface of his desk. "Take that, Torch Boy. She's going out with me on Valentine's Day."

"Are you all right?"

Will looked up, his chin still resting on his desk. Mrs. Arnstein stood in the door, gracing him with a grim smile. "I'm fine. I thought you'd left."

"I was waiting for the travel agency to deliver your tickets for Denver," she said, stepping inside to place the plane ticket on his desk. "You fly out Monday morning and come back on Saturday afternoon. Do you want me to call a car to drive you to the airport?"

Will sat up straight. "I thought I was coming back Friday. Saturday is Valentine's Day."

"They called to change the Friday meeting with the architects to a dinner meeting. They said it would go well into the night and I couldn't get a flight for Saturday morning. I didn't realize you had plans for Valentine's Day."

"I should be fine. And I'll take my own car to and from O'Hare."

"Will there be anything else?" she asked.

"Yeah. Do you know a good place to go dancing in this city? I'm not talking about a disco-type club with lights and a DJ. I want a place where they have a real dance band that plays romantic, old-fashioned music. A place where people slow dance."

Mrs. Arnstein grinned. "Old-fashioned music? I don't know of any places offhand. Mr. Arnstein isn't

particularly light on his feet so we've never been much
for dancing. But I can call around and find out. Are you
planning to take someone dancing on Valentine's
Day?''

"Maybe," Will said.

"Then, I'll get on it right away."

She walked out of the office and Will leaned back in
his leather chair, linking his hands behind his head.
Dinner was easy. He had regular tables at a number of
trendy Chicago restaurants. Dancing was in the works.
"Flowers," Will murmured. "English roses, of course.
A big bouquet in cream and yellow." Was there anything he'd missed?

Will reached into his jacket pocket and pulled out
the small velvet box he'd taken to carrying around
with him. He opened it and pulled out the diamond
ring. A few weeks ago, he'd thought the purchase had
been just a stupid mistake, a waste of money. But for
the first time since Jane had walked out on him, he had
reason to hope the ring might someday find its way
onto her finger.

"THIS IS THE SECOND TIME we've done this and I didn't
like it much the first time," Lisa complained.

Jane grabbed a grocery bag from the back seat of
Lisa's car and dropped it into her friend's arms. "I just
need you to help me carry all this in. Then you can be
on your way without having participated in any
crime."

Grudgingly, Lisa followed Jane up the front steps of
Will's house. "How do you know he's not home?"

"I called his office and his secretary said he's coming

back on a flight from Denver at three. That means I have at least an hour to get dinner started, fix up the house and change before he gets home."

"I have to say, Janie, this is really a romantic idea."

"It's going to be great. I bought some new CDs with really romantic music. And I've got champagne and strawberries. And I bought five hundred dollars worth of scented candles. I'm going to light the entire first floor with candles. It'll be so beautiful."

"You can't afford rent, but you spent five hundred dollars on candles?"

"If this works, I won't need to worry about rent."

Lisa's eyebrow rose. "What about the bedroom? Candlelight is always good when one is about to get naked."

"The bedroom," Jane said with a soft laugh. "Well, I'm not going to count on that. But I'll save a few just in case." Jane unlocked the front door and quickly stepped inside to turn off the security system. She expected to find Thurgood waiting, then realized the dog was probably staying elsewhere while Will was out of town. In truth, she was relieved. Thurgood would not be ruining another holiday. Jane walked to the kitchen and set the groceries down on the counter, then opened the refrigerator. It hadn't taken Will long to revert to his bachelor lifestyle. There was nothing in the fridge but beer and a loaf of bread.

"I'll go get the rest of the stuff from the car," Lisa said. "What are you making for dinner?"

"I was going to make liver," Jane said, "just as a nod to our first meal together. But instead, I'm making tournedos of beef with a red wine and shallot glaze.

And Potatoes Anna. And fresh green beans. And I bought a chocolate cheesecake for dessert.''

''You really love this guy, don't you?''

Jane paused from unpacking the groceries and considered the question. ''Yes, I do. For so long, I didn't want to risk my heart. I was certain if I let myself love him, then he'd somehow find a way to leave me. But I'm not afraid of that anymore. I want to take the chance and see where this goes. He made the first move asking me out for Valentine's Day. Now I'm making the next.''

''Are you going to tell him about Prince Charming?''

''I am. I think he deserves to know the truth. If it scares him off, then so be it. We started a relationship on such shaky ground with that silly contract. If we're going to begin all over again, I want it to be the right way.''

Lisa stepped up to Jane's side and gave her a fierce hug. ''I'm so happy for you. This is like a fairy tale come true. You've loved this man since you met him and now you're going to have him.''

''I think I am,'' Jane murmured.

Lisa brushed a tear from her cheek, then hurried back out to the car to retrieve the rest of the groceries. When she'd brought everything inside, Jane and Lisa unwrapped the candles and placed them around the house, lighting them as they went along. Within fifteen minutes, the warm smell of vanilla filled every room. Once they had finished preparations in the kitchen, Jane decided to build a fire before changing. When the logs crackled in the family-room fireplace, she stepped back and drew a deep breath. "That's it," she said. "There's nothing else I can do here but wait."

"What if he doesn't come home? What if he comes straight to our apartment to pick you up?"

"Then you'll have to tell him where I am. But I think he'll come home first."

Lisa gave Jane a quick hug. "Good luck. I swear, this is just the most romantic Valentine's Day ever."

Jane sent her friend a little wave as she walked out, then turned back to the kitchen. Though she'd felt pretty confident up until now, her stomach suddenly clenched into a nervous knot. She recognized the feeling, that oddly sick but exhilarating sensation she'd experienced the very first time she'd met Will McCaffrey—and every time she'd seen him since then.

A glance at her watch gave her only ten minutes before Will should be home. She grabbed the garment bag that held her clothes and hurried upstairs to the bathroom.

She'd chosen an outfit that was deliberately sexy, a clingy black cashmere sweater and a leather mini. "I know," she murmured to herself, smoothing her hands over the skirt and adjusting the deeply cut neckline. "Tight sweater. Leather. It's a cheap trick, but I've got to go for it." The black silk stockings and three-inch pumps completed the look. Jane dabbed a bit of perfume on her wrists and between her breasts and decided that she'd done all she could. The rest was up to Will.

Suddenly, she heard the security system beep. Someone was coming in the door. Jane drew a deep breath, closed her eyes and said a little prayer. Then she stepped out of the bathroom and hurried down the stairs.

When she got to the kitchen, Will was standing at the stove, still wearing his overcoat and peering into the oven with a confused frown on his face. He held a bouquet of flowers in his hand. English roses. "Hi," she said.

He spun around and the moment he saw her, he smiled. "What is this?"

"It's dinner. After liver and onions and the Thanksgiving fiasco, I figured I owed you a decent meal."

His grin widened as he took a step toward her. "I had big plans for this evening. Dinner, dancing." He held out the bouquet. "Flowers."

"Thank you," Jane smiled, taking the flowers from his hand. "They're my favorites."

"I know."

"I know you know." Jane pushed up on her toes and gave him a quick kiss, but as she drew away, his gaze fixed on her mouth. She waited, frozen in time, and then it happened. In one smooth motion, Will swept her into his arms and kissed her, thoroughly and completely, his lips taking possession of hers, his tongue softly invading. By the time the kissed ended, Jane was breathless and completely flustered. She opened her mouth to speak, but she couldn't think of anything to say.

"I suppose I should have waited for that," Will said, a devilish grin twitching at his lips. "But I've been thinking about kissing you since the last time I saw you, and I'm not a patient man."

"I've been thinking about kissing you, too," Jane admitted, her face warm with the excitement.

"You have?"

She nodded. "Maybe we could do that again?"

He stared down at her, then shook his head. "Nope, not yet."

"No?"

"Before I kiss you again, I need to know what happened with Torch Boy."

"Who is Torch Boy?"

"That guy you've been carrying a torch for. I need to know where I stand here, Janie. If this guy is still waiting on the sidelines, then this isn't going to happen for us. I'm not going to compete for your affections. Either you love me one hundred percent or we don't see each other until you can."

She nodded slowly. "All right. I understand that."

"So how do you feel about him?"

"I love him," Jane said. "I've loved him for a long time. When I first met him, I thought he was the most wonderful man in the world. And then we were apart for a few years and I still loved him. I used to dream that we'd meet on the street one day. And not too long ago, that dream came true."

Realization slowly began to dawn on Will's face. "And what happened then?" he asked in a wary tone.

"Well, it got a little messy. There was this contract and our families and I got scared. I was afraid if I loved him too much, he'd leave me."

Will narrowed his eyes and sent her an incredulous look. "I'm Torch Boy?"

"Yeah. When you're not Slave Boy."

He chuckled softly, then burst into a deep laugh. "I'm Torch Boy. *I'm* the one you love?"

"You are. And I do love you, Will. I've always loved you."

His hands slipped up to her face, cupping her cheeks and pulling her into another kiss, this one slow and languid and filled with promise.

"I love you, too, Janie." He stared down into her eyes, his fingers skimming her face as if he wanted to take in every detail of her expression. "I know I loved you long before I actually realized it. I loved you when we were friends in college, but I was too stupid to see it. And then when you came to live here, I loved you even more, but I tried to force you to feel the same way and you got scared. Now, I just love you, Jane. Plain and simple. And forever."

Jane nuzzled her face into his chest, the cashmere overcoat soft on her skin. "I don't know what to say. What are you supposed say when all your dreams come true?"

"Yes," Will replied.

"Yes?"

He stepped back from her and brushed his coat aside, then reached into his jacket pocket. Jane's breath caught in her throat when she saw the familiar velvet box in the palm of his hand. He opened it and withdrew the ring, then took her fingers in his. "Say 'yes,'" he murmured, his gaze skimming her face, searching her eyes for the answer before she said it. "Marry me, Janie."

Jane bit her bottom lip, trying to stem the flood of

tears that threatened. She drew a ragged breath and nodded. "Yes."

One word was all it took to erase the mistakes of the past and to open up the door to their future. Will slipped the ring onto her finger, then grabbed her waist and spun her around and around. Their laughter mingled with the sounds of a Celine Dion love song playing on the stereo.

Jane had always wondered why Valentine's Day had been such a depressing holiday for her, why it never turned out to match her fantasies. But now she knew. Fate was saving one very special Valentine's Day just for her, a day she could tuck away in her memory and savor for the rest of her life. A day when she finally found the man of her dreams. A day when that man finally realized that Jane Singleton was the woman of his dreams.

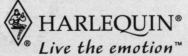

If you enjoyed what you just read,
then we've got an offer you can't resist!

Take 2 bestselling love stories FREE!

Plus get a FREE surprise gift!